RUN HOLLY RUN

WALTER ROUZER

Run Holly Run

Copyright © 2009 by Walter Rouzer

Peak Wave Publishing
peakwave.org

ISBN 978-0-9970304-1-9

Author contact: http://www. wrouzer.com

TO WALLY, PAM, JESSICA,
KIMBERLY AND IRIS

PROLOGUE

Dark clouds and rumblings of thunder brewed into a wicked storm over the small town of Kingston.

Suddenly, without warning, a giant beam of light flashed down from the eye of the storm, leaving in its wake a huge circle of burnt earth in the center of a cornfield. Neither blade of grass nor sprout of weed ever grew back in that spot again.

Everyone in town agreed that the four-hundred-foot wide circle in Bellarouse and Mitchell Haggerty's cornfield was much more than a freak of nature. Some went so far as to say it was out of this world... even supernatural.

* * * * *

"Get away from my property!" shouted Bellarouse at the two boys standing on the opposite side of her fence. A moment later, she burst out the back door. "That pig! That gluttonous, potbellied ogre! Button Rouge has been in my vegetable patch again! Hasn't he!"

Mitch and Shane dropped their ball and bat and backed away from the fence.

Just minutes earlier, something strange had happened to their friend, Albert Drusky, after he'd chased his pet pig, Button Rouge, into Bellarouse's cornfield. After they both disappeared amongst the cornstalks, Mitch and Shane called out over and over again for their friend to come out, but there was only silence. Seconds later, they were startled seeing two beams of red light flash out from the midst of the field. At that same instant, they'd heard a scream followed by a loud squeal.

The next moment, Button Rouge exploded out from the field like a cannonball—greased lightning—flying fifteen feet through the air before bouncing on his belly among the cornstalks, not far from where the two boys stood. The pig dove underneath the fence, digging and scrambling to squeeze his way back to the other side. He stopped for a moment, eyes turned inward, staring at its huge nose. He shook its head like he was in shock, then ran up to Mitch and Shane and tugged on their pant legs with his teeth, squealing loudly, trying to tell them what had happened—that he was really Albert, not Button Rouge, the castaway pig. But all they could hear were snorts and squeals.

"Get away, pig!" said Mitch, looking very irritated. Albert the pig raced across the lawn and up the back steps to the Druskys' nearby house, then took a flying leap through the screen door.

Just outside, Bellarouse's eyes bulged wide at the two boys. "You! Did you let that pig loose?" she hollered, pointing at her vegetable patch.

Mitch and Shane backed away from the fence, then suddenly ran toward the Druskys' house.

Bellarouse discovered two sets of fresh tracks leading into her cornfield—one human, the other pig. "Trespassers! Filthy pigs!" she snarled, stomping into the field after the intruders.

* * * * *

Inside the Druskys' house, Albert stopped just short of the kitchen entrance and listened to the spattering of bacon grease in an iron skillet. He normally liked bacon, but now the smell made him feel squeamish. He could see his mother, Annabel, chopping carrots on the island counter. He slowly walked up to her heels and let out a loud squeal. The noise startled Annabel so much she shot straight up. The next moment, Albert saw her staring back down at him with squinty eyes.

"Button! Button Rouge!" she shouted, wagging her finger at him, "Get out of this kitchen!" She pointed toward the broken back door. "Look what you did. Get out of this house, right now!"

Albert just stood motionless, looking up, wishing by some miracle she would recognize him as her son, beneath the pig fat. He made snorts and squeals trying in his clearest voice to let her know that he wasn't Button Rouge, the pig, but Albert.

Annabel became distracted a moment, hearing the front door buzzer sound off over and over again. She ignored the doorbell and quickly refocused her attention on Button Rouge.

"What be the matter with you… pig?" she yelled, with a distinct emphasis on the last word.

When Albert heard that, his beady eyes instantly swelled up with tears.

Annabel stormed out of the kitchen, then reappeared seconds later holding a leash.

At that same moment, just outside on the front porch, Mitch and Shane began pounding their fists on the front door. They were worried sick about Albert's disappearance, and Bellarouse's threatening remarks. They didn't even want to think about what might happen if she caught him in her field.

Annabel heard the pounding coming from the front door, but remained focused on the pig. She chased Albert in a game of ring-around-the-kitchen-island. He made a sharp turn out of the kitchen and darted down the hallway.

Annabel chased right after the pig. Suddenly, Albert heard her stop dead in her tracks. She must have remembered that the stovetop was on high— even he could hear grease spattering in the iron skillet. One thing she hated more than a dirty farm animal inside her house, he knew, was a kitchen with grease all over the stove and floor. She ran back and turned off the stove, then took a white rag and started wiping grease off the burner and floor.

This gave Albert a chance to think for a moment about what to do next. His pig brain swirled in hyper-drive. How can I convince my mom that I'm really her son? he thought.

He looked upstairs toward his bedroom, then toward the family room and piano. An idea flashed in his mind that might give him a chance to convince his mom that he was at least more than just a run-of-the-mill pig.

He dashed into the family room and took a flying leap onto the piano bench. He pressed all four of his little toes onto the cushion as hard as he could to keep from sliding off the other end. Next, he wiggled onto his pink bottom and nudged the piano cover open with his snout. His legs stuck straight out. Albert used the tips of his front feet to work the keys. With each tap, a note of hope filled his ears.

Just inside the kitchen, Annabel's rag slipped through her fingers to the floor. It sounded as if her son was playing the piano. She stopped what she was doing and quickly headed into the living room, then stared at the pig with her jaw hanging wide open in a mixed state of shock and amusement.

Albert was determined to give his best performance, playing the music as perfectly as he could. Although he couldn't speak or hum, he could still squeal and snort. His eyes lit up like sparklers, seeing he had his mom's full attention.

He tried to make himself look like Albert, but it just wasn't working out the way he wanted. He could see his mom's eyes narrowing more and more with each passing second. Albert looked back at his mom smiling, trying to sing and tap all the right piano keys with his front feet. His butt wiggled from side to side as he tried his best to play all the right notes. His corkscrew tail twitched up and down, round and about. All of a sudden, his face flushed pink as he noticed dirt flaking off his body, landing on her new carpet. Annabel saw it too, and the sight kindled her temper. She raced right toward him with her leash in hand. Albert took a flying leap off the bench, then took off running toward the stairs. The wood floor had recently been waxed. His feet slipped out from underneath him, and he went sliding across the floor up against the door.

That same moment, out on the front porch, Mitch and Shane heard a loud thud against the door as they continued to press the buzzer, and rap their knuckles against the wood.

Albert scurried upstairs on all fours, keeping his focus on the finish line, which was the safe haven of his bed. His only hope was to go undercover before it was too late.

Albert's sister, Meagan, popped her head out

of her bedroom door and was shocked to see a pig running up the stairs. She couldn't believe her eyes! "A pig, Mom! A dirty filthy pig is running loose in the house! You know how I hate pigs!"

Albert stopped in front of his room and squinted back at Meagan.

"Filthy, dirty pig!" she yelled down the hallway. Albert let out the loudest squeal he could muster at Meagan before he disappeared inside his room. He quickly backed into the door, slamming it shut. Gazing about the room, he felt so small and isolated, so alone. His heart weighed heavily upon him. A sudden idea flashed in his head. He ran over to a large stuffed bear that was sitting by the side of the room, then grabbed the bear's arm in his teeth and flung it onto the bed. Next, he went to the far corner of his room and ran as fast as he could, making a flying leap onto the bed. He pulled the covers back with his teeth, then covered the bear with the cotton sheet before jumping down and hiding between the bed and wall.

Seconds later, he heard the door open. Annabel saw a large lump under the covers. "How'd you get yourself under the covers like that? You'd better get out of that bed, right now!"

Annabel couldn't understand why he wasn't moving, so she reached down and threw back the covers. "What this?" she screeched, seeing the stuffed bear. She leaned over the side of the bed and discovered Albert's hiding place.

"So there you are!" she scowled.

Before he had the chance to back out from between the bed, he felt the collar slip over his head, then tighten snugly around his neck. He didn't want to go out without a fight so he sat with his butt to the floor unwilling to move.

"Come on now! Come on! Let's get going!" said Annabel tugging him forward.

Albert grimaced as he felt his butt slide across the hallway floor. On his way downstairs, he heard pounding and knocking by the front door.

"What's all the racket, boys?" asked Annabel when she finally looked outside.

Albert saw his two buddies looking up at his mom, appearing really worried.

"Albert chased Button Rouge into Haggertys' field and never came back out!"said Shane.

Annabel handed him the leash. "You get Button back into his pen while I check on Albert."

Shane pulled and tugged the pig toward the barn. Albert felt like a fugitive being sent to prison— pig row. I've got to make a break for it and get my body back. I've got to! I've got to! He suddenly stopped, refusing to take one more step.

"Come on, Button," coaxed Shane. "Come on!" he said, tugging on the leash.

Albert looked up at his friend with narrowed eyes, then suddenly burst out running in the opposite direction. Shane flew sideways and was dragged across the ground a few feet before he let go of the leash. Albert darted out around the house, then suddenly skidded to a stop, seeing Bellarouse stomping around her backyard with an angry look on her face.

CHAPTER 1

Two Weeks Later

Holly Atwood headed south along a dirt road that hugged the Mississippi River. Squinting out into the distance, she spotted the McGuire mansion she and her parents had just moved into; a grey stone castle located on a grassy knoll overlooking the river.

A steamboat suddenly appeared downstream and got close enough that Holly could see it in detail. The captain yelled out, "More fuel! More fuel!" Two men covered with black soot hurriedly shoveled coal into the broiler, sending fire and smoke up through its seventy-foot high stacks. The captain stared out the window with his eyes fixed on the mansion, then suddenly shifted his attention toward Holly— a tom girl wearing baggy jeans and a blue striped shirt. Holly couldn't help but wonder why the steamer sped up as it neared the mansion, then suddenly slowed down once it passed.

Squinting out in the distance, Holly caught sight of a flicker of light coming from the mansion's attic window. The flame grew brighter and brighter until she could make out the stark white faces of two girls. They appeared to be twins, and couldn't have been more than ten or twelve. A haunting whisper arose from the attic window that sounded like cries for help. Holly took a deep swallow. There wasn't supposed to be anyone else living in the mansion besides herself and her parents.

The light in the attic window suddenly disappeared, and the ghostly faces of the twins vanished before her eyes. Everything fell silent. Not even a solitary cricket could be heard. Moments later, the sounds of the crickets once again filled the air. Holly stared intently toward the attic window, but the light didn't return. The eerie cries were gone.

A thick fog rolled in across the river, catching her by surprise. Moments later, she heard what sounded like swift footsteps coming her way.

"Who is it? Who's there?" she shouted. All of a sudden, a young man raced past her wearing a green beret. What's his big hurry? she thought.

When Holly reached the McGuire mansion she stopped and stared up toward the attic. A shaft of moonlight illuminated a rusted lantern sitting on the windowsill.

There must be a way to get up there, she

thought. She shifted her attention toward the front of the mansion and tried to think of a way to get back inside without her parents noticing.

Heading across the grounds, she passed beneath giant oak trees. Their branches arched over the circular driveway that led to the front of the mansion. Holly scurried past a marble cherubim standing by the front steps. The arrow and heart it once held now lay as broken pieces at the base of its feet. She knelt by the front window. The ground beneath her knees felt soggy, the result of a series of thunderstorms passing through earlier in the day.

She peered through a side window and saw her parents, Phyllis and Patrick, sitting together on a black leather couch next to the stone fireplace. A low fire burned in the grate. She saw her mom get up from the couch and head across the front entranceway, then stop and peer inside one of the side rooms. The window was cracked open just enough so she could hear them when they spoke.

"Just perfect," Phyllis remarked, removing art supplies from a packing box at the base of the stairs.

Holly thought it might be too difficult to sneak back inside through the front door. I'm going to be so busted with extra chores if they catch me, she thought. She made her way around to the back of the mansion, then pulled, tugged, and jiggled all the doors and windows. It was to no avail; they were all secured and locked. She crawled on her hands and knees up to the front window again. She saw her dad sitting by the fireplace, leaning forward, with his long thin hands clasped together. His head hung low, as if in deep thought, eyes focused on the flicker of flame. He stretched his open palms toward the heat. The fire was burning low, and the charcoal began to crackle and pop as it cooled. Phyllis walked over to Patrick and gazed up at a large framed photo hanging above the fireplace; a replica of a hundred year old black-and-white photograph taken of the ten-year-old McGuire twins, Stephanie and Agatha. Sitting on either side of the girls were their two Great Danes. The dogs had huge pointy ears and shiny coats. The picture showed one of the dogs with its muzzle pressed softly against the girl's cheek.

"What a happy moment in time that must have been," said Phyllis, gazing up at the picture. "Patrick, darling?" she said, leaning forward, giving him a big hug. "Honey, can you help me move this photo into my new art studio?"

"Absolutely!" he replied. He got up from the sofa and helped her carry the photo of the twins into her newly set up art studio so she could get started with her painting. She was commissioned by Bret McGuire, grandson to the mansion's original owner, Morgan McGuire, to renovate the black-and-white photo. Phyllis had a special talent for making old photos look come alive with her colorful oil paints.

"Now's my chance," whispered Holly to herself,

seeing the coast was clear. She opened the front door just enough to slip inside, then tiptoed toward the stairway, all the while hoping the crackle coming from the fire would mask the sound of her footsteps. When she got about halfway up the stairs, the sound of her father's voice rang out from behind.

"Holly! Your mother and I have been worried sick about you! Where have you been?" said Patrick, squinting at her from across the foyer.

I'm so busted, she thought. She looked back into her father's eyes. A blank expression hung on her face in a moment of silence. "Well, Dad, I..."

Phyllis stepped alongside Patrick. They walked up to the foot of the stairs, crossing their arms in front of them in unison.

"Holly, dear, where have you been?" said Phyllis, staring up at her with her pointy nose and black rimmed glasses.

"Oh, just outside, hanging out by the river."

Patrick sighed, "Sometimes you can be so mysterious and secretive. I really get worried about you on occasions like this."

Phyllis took a step forward. "Holly, dear, we just moved here, and don't know what's lurking about by that river, especially at night."

Patrick spoke up, "You know, sweetheart, your disappearing act just cost you a new cleaning job." He pointed toward an unpacked box at the base of the stairs with a toilet plunger sticking halfway out.

"One of the toilets is in need of a fix. The bathroom in question is just down that hallway to your right."

Holly shook her head as she pulled out the plunger. She stopped for a moment in front of her mom's studio and watched her organize tubes of oil paint in neat rows.

"Mom, I'm taking the plunge… I don't know if I'll make it back. You know I can't hold my breath that long." She pretended to cough.

"I believe in you, Holly darling," giving her a thumbs-up. "You can accomplish anything in life."

Holly held the plunger limply at her side. "Yeah…right…the last time I did this kind of work my face got flushed!"

A short time later, after successfully completing her task, Holly headed back upstairs and stopped in front of the chained and padlocked double doors to the master suite. She remembered hearing rumors that the room had been sealed shut for over a hundred years.

The doors were made of black mahogany, kept shiny by several coats of lacquer. Holly got down on her hands and knees, then pressed her ear up against the place where the doors met, listening for any heartbeat of life, sounds of movement— clanking of a chain, burst of wind, or flapping curtains. She sensed a restless force lurking inside and was determined to unlock its secrets.

Holly jumped, hearing her father suddenly call

out to her from downstairs.

"Are you expecting to find something in that room? You know it's been sealed shut for over a century. There's nothing in there. Nothing!"

"Dad... how do you know what's in there if it's been sealed for a hundred years?" She gripped the iron padlock and gave it a sharp yank.

"Holly!" said Patrick, sounding more irritated. His right hand gripped the wrought iron railing.

"Yes, Dad?" she said, giving him her full attention.

"Perhaps you've forgotten that one of the conditions for our staying here is that we never go into that room. Don't you suppose that's why it has a huge lock on it."

"But, Dad... what's with the big secret?"

"It's not for us to ask."

"What would it matter if we knew, and they didn't?"

Patrick sighed and headed back to his study room.

Holly stepped over to a side window, then leaned out, trying to catch a glimpse of the attic. She was startled to see the rusted lantern on the windowsill spark a flicker of light that quickly grew brighter and brighter, until it beamed like a lighthouse out across the river toward an approaching steamboat. Holly's eyes bulged wide, seeing the stark white faces of two girls suddenly appear on either side of the lantern.

They had chestnut hair tied with yellow ribbons and wore red and white plaid dresses with puffy sleeves. They were same twins she remembered seeing in the picture downstairs, but that was impossible, for she was told that they mysteriously disappeared well over a hundred years ago.

The twins gazed down at the strange girl inhabiting their home. Holly was so shaken by their appearance and piercing stare, she lost her sense of balance and slipped over the window's ledge. A frightful nightmare of falling through space enveloped her. She looked straight up as she fell and saw the light of the lantern and the twins' faces blur before her.

She landed on the squishy, rain soaked grass below, softening her otherwise treacherous fall. With the wind knocked out of her, her stomach was in knots. She sucked in a gasp of air as stars danced before her eyes.

She gripped her shoulder and groaned, then touched her hip. Grimacing, she rocked her waist and shoulders from side-to-side, then took a deep sigh of relief, feeling as if nothing was broken. Dazed and unsteady, she stared up toward the attic. It was pitch black, with no signs of the twins, and no flicker of light. Holly tried her best to enter the house again unnoticed. She tiptoed across the front entrance and made it about halfway up the stairs before she heard her dad's voice.

"Holly!" said Patrick, "How did you get outside again?"

Holly sighed and took a deep breath, "Well Dad… as a matter of fact I…" but she quickly fell silent, knowing all too well that neither of her parents believed in ghostly appearances. She continued upstairs, then down the hallway to her bedroom. There must be another way to get into the attic, she thought. Holly was determined to find a way to meet the twins face-to-face, no matter what dangers might be lurking about within the mansion's walls.

CHAPTER 2

At dawn, Phyllis slipped out of bed and headed down the hallway to the mansion's floating stairway. It jutted out from the wall and waved like a rollercoaster, going down, leveling off, then down again. The carpet was faded, once crimson red, now a washed-out pink. Phyllis stopped at the bottom of the stairs a moment and yawned. Her slippers dragged across the white marble floor as she crossed the foyer. Upon entering her art studio, she felt an eerie silence. Something just wasn't right. The air smelled musty, stagnant, unlike the day before. She walked over to the far end of the room and opened the shutters. The sunlight lifted her mood from the mansion's gloomy hues of gray and black.

She stared across the room toward the painting of the McGuire twins and their dogs. From a distance, everything she had worked on the day before looked exactly the same as she had left it. Phyllis sat down and squeezed paint onto her palette, blending the colors together to add life to the flower gardens. She poised her brush over the canvas, ready to make the first strokes when she stopped dead in her tracks. Her brush slipped from her fingers and fell to the floor. She shook her head and rubbed her eyes, then placed a magnifying glass over the images.

"No, it can't be," she muttered. The happy expressions she had so tenderly brought to life with vivid color the day before had vanished. She leaned forward to get a closer look. Her fingers began to tremble, moisture building on the palms of her hands.

Gone were her restorative brush strokes depicting soft innocence and youth. The once blushing cheeks of the twins were now grey, and their eyes were encircled by purple smudges. As for the dogs, the rich-textured hues of brown she had painted onto their fur to reflect their shiny coats now appeared dull. Their muscular forms had disappeared, replaced by skin and bone.

Phyllis's eyes narrowed in anger. Who could have possibly done this horrible thing by changing my painting like this? Certainly not Patrick or Holly. But, if not them, then who? Perhaps someone broke into the house last night and did this. She left her studio and moved from room to room, checking all the doors and windows. They were all secure and locked. She felt relieved, but, at the same, more puzzled. How could this have happened? she thought. She tried to pull herself together by taking some deep breaths to relax, then went back to work, restoring the appearance of the twins and the dogs to the way they were the day before.

Later That Day

Holly entered the front gate to the Robinson Estate at 78 Canterbury Drive, located on a high plateau overlooking the Mississippi River. As she made her way across the white cobblestone pathway leading to the front door, she inhaled the sweet fragrance of jasmine and gardenia blossoms. The flowers thrived in the neatly kept garden. Holly pulled back the brass lion's head doorknocker, then released it, making a loud rap. Seconds later, Mr. Burt Robinson opened the door holding his pet pug, Puddles, snugly in his arms. It is said, in some cases, dog owners' faces in some ways resemble their pets, and Burt was no exception.

"Hi, I'm Holly," she said with a wide grin, "Um… may I please speak to Charlie?"

"Regarding?" said Burt, taking notice her large almond shaped eyes and red highlighted shoulder length hair.

"He called me." She leaned sideways and stared curiously around his shoulder.

"You must be one of his new friends. Don't recall seeing you about?"

"We attend the same school and are on the debate team."

"That "Truth Busters" group?"

"You got it. Guess there aren't too many secrets around here."

Burt looked back over his shoulder toward the top of the stairs. "Charlie, your friend, Holly, is here."

"Great! Tell her I'll be right down!"

"Well, just don't stand there," said Burt, "Come inside."

Charlie headed downstairs wearing a green beret, blue jeans, and red letterman football jacket. "Can Holly and I have some privacy… in your study?"

"Charlie, really…"

"Seriously, Dad, can we have some privacy, please?"

He hesitated. "Well… all right, since I have to take Puddles to the vet."

Charlie's twelve-year-old brother, Kent, appeared down the hallway and walked up to the front door with his mom, Helen, following right behind.

Burt slipped Puddles into his son's arms. Kent had plump cheeks and thick inch-high brown hair trimmed flat across the top.

"Mom," said Charlie, "I'd like to introduce you to my new friend, Holly."

Helen stepped up to the new guest. "It's a pleasure to meet you, Holly."

"Likewise," she replied, taking note of her tall, thin frame, billowy blond hair and retro looking polka-dot dress.

After the introductions, Burt, Helen, Kent, and Puddles headed out the front door to the car.

With the house now to themselves, Charlie and Holly entered Burt's large office suite and sat next to each other on the leather couch.

"By the way," said Charlie, "what part of Kingston did you move too?"

"East side. We're staying at the McGuire mansion."

"The McGuire's! Hum…I hate to say it, but I think that place might be haunted."

"Haunted?"

Charlie's eyes stretched wide. "You dig dead people?"

"Good one, Charlie," she replied, gazing into his piercing eyes. This guy is kind of funny, she thought. She leaned forward. "A man by the name of Bret McGuire made the arrangements for us to stay there. He commissioned my mom to oil paint a black-and-white photograph that hung above the fireplace."

"Don't want to get you too worried," said Charlie, "but rumor has it that the lady who lived there before you went crazy. They say the paintings did it to her."

"How?"

"The ghosts. They say they communicate by making changes in the painting."

She shook her head. "Really… very interesting, but hard to believe."

Charlie noticed Holly kept staring at his hat. "Do you find my hat really interesting?" He tilted his head to one side with a slight grin.

"Why?"

"You haven't taken your eyes off it since you came in here."

This guy is really cute, but kind of self-conscious. Holly cleared her throat. "Your hat looks… something… well… very familiar." Her eyebrows suddenly arched. "Now I remember. A guy came bursting out of the fog and scared the willies out of me last night while I was checking out the river. He went by so fast the only thing I could make out was that he was wearing a green beret that looked just like yours."

Charlie's lips curved into a mischievous grin. "I can't tell a lie. It was me."

"What?" said Holly, squinting.

"It was me," he repeated, sliding his hat off.

"It's okay," she said, "The night was dark, the mist thick. It happened so fast we didn't get the chance to recognize each other. That's OK. Just curious though. Why were you running down that road last night in such a mad rush? Running from what?"

"I heard some wild screeching coming from inside my Uncle Melvin's shack located about a mile down river from where I passed you. Nightmare went flying out the window and leapt right at me! Acted like he was trying to keep me out for some reason."

"Wait, wait, wait. Slow down," said Holly, raising her palms. "Who's Nightmare?"

"Uncle Melvin's cat."

"Nightmare?" What a weird name for a cat, she thought. "What were you doing out by that shack?"

"I brought some food for the poor creature. He lives there alone now. Still can't believe Melvin's gone. He disappeared without a trace." Charlie fell silent.

Holly noticed his left hand start to twitch nervously. "What about the police… the sheriff?"

"They couldn't find anything."

"Tell me more about this cat."

"Did you ever have a really bad nightmare; like when you woke up in the middle of the night in a cold sweat?"

"Sweat? Not like that," said Holly.

"Look at it another way. Think of your worst nightmare. When you see this cat it will all come back to you."

"That bad, huh?"

"Yeah. I'm not kidding." He reached out and placed his hand on her shoulder. "Just to give you a sneak mental preview, he's a big black tomcat with a freaky scar in the shape of an X on his forehead."

"Wow!" That cat must have got into some wicked fight, she thought.

"For the other details, I'll let you discover them for yourself."

"Can't wait to meet this cat in person."

"You're daring," said Charlie, clearly impressed with her valor.

"Why is Nightmare living out there all by himself? Can't you find a temporary home till they find your Uncle Melvin?"

"I tried to find him a nice place to stay, but he keeps on escaping, then hightails it right back to the cabin. Won't leave. Loves Uncle Melvin to death."

"Is there anything else that's been happening around town that strikes you as being unusual?"

"As a matter of fact, yes. Things started to turn really bizarre around town after my Aunt Bellarouse started her pet-sitting business a few weeks ago. She hired me to take care of some of her client's pets. Lately I've been noticing that when the people have been away for a day or two, and come back, they're not the same. It's like their personalities left. Pretty much, it seems as though they become like strangers. And their pets. They're acting really weird too."

"In what way?"

"They become super smart and do things their

owners liked to do. For example, a resident by the name of Mr. Roth would always play chess with his poodle on his lap. The last time I saw him, his dog had his bottom feet on the chair with his front legs on the table. And get this. He was moving chess pieces around the board with his nose."

"And Mr. Roth—what was he doing?"

"He was just sitting on the couch staring and smiling at his dog like... like he was being entertained."

"Sounds like the twilight zone. Tell me more about this aunt. What's she like?"

"Very big, and very aggressive. And did I mention...mysterious...bizarre? Her husband, Mitchell, just recently disappeared too. I only see her daughter now, Marie. She's ten. You won't believe this, but Bellarouse bought her daughter a handmade guillotine for her last birthday. A month later, I saw Marie out in the garden with a shovel digging holes."

"Holes?"

"She was making a graveyard. Fifty holes for the bodies!"

"Oh my gosh! Whose bodies?"

"Her headless doll collection!"

Holly, eyes stretched wide. "That's super crazy and spooky." That moment she wondered what a ten-year-old would look like in a straightjacket. She looked blankly to one side for a moment in silence, then glanced back into Charlie's piercing, deep set eyes. "Can you remember the approximate time when the people started to disappear and the pets and owners began acting really weird?"

Charlie raised his finger to his broad chin and thought for a moment. "Yes. I think it all started about a month ago, after we had a freaky storm. I was in my bedroom when it struck. I heard the dishes downstairs falling off onto the floor, crashing… shattering. The noise became louder and louder until it almost sounded like a steamroller crashing through the house."

"Wow!" said Holly.

"Yeah, and get this…a giant beam of light flashed down from the eye of the storm and shook the whole town!"

"Was there anything else? Tell-tale signs in the aftermath?"

"Yes, as a matter of fact, it left a huge four-hundred-foot black circle in the middle of my aunt Bellarouse's cornfield."

"I'd like to check that place out. How about five o'clock tomorrow? Can you make it?"

"Are you sure you want to go out there?" said Charlie, casting a worried look. "I already told you what my aunt is like."

"Yep. We can be really stealthy. I can give you some pointers. She'll never know we were there. I'm just really curious about that place."

"You really are daring, aren't you? And did I mention sneaky?"

"A passion of mine is to bring to light the facts that make interesting mystery cases. As they say, leave no stone unturned. Do you by chance have a map of Kingston?"

Charlie got up from the couch. "Better yet, I have an aerial map of the whole town and surrounding area." He retrieved his dad's map from his desk drawer, then laid it out across the glass coffee table. He pointed toward the top left section. "Here's your place, the McGuire mansion, and over there is where my house is located."

"That's interesting," said Holly, spotting six large mansions on the map. She noticed they were all located on a high four-mile wide arching bluff that ran along the eastern part of town. Each mansion had a beautiful view of the river and surrounding farmland. Holly took note that the McGuire mansion was the one closest to the river.

Charlie slid his finger across to a different section of the map. "This southwest portion of town is mostly farmland," he said, "comprised of twenty-acres lots, all shaped like piano keys butting up against each other. The eastern end of the farms all face the bank of the Mississippi. From an aerial view looking down, each lot appears a different color, ranging from green to brown depending on whether they're used for grass crops like alfalfa or for watermelons, orchards, even livestock, horses, pigs, and other farm animals. All the farms have big barns to shelter their animals and other buildings for storing and processing crops."

"Can you point out to me where your aunt's house is? And Melvin's cabin?"

"Sure." He slid his finger across the map. "Here's Bellarouse's house and farm, four lots down from the others, near the county line. The cornfield is toward the back of her property." He pointed to a very small structure located on the banks of the Mississippi, about a mile down the road from Bellarouse's farm. "This is where my Uncle Melvin's cabin is located."

"Charlie, do you think your dad would mind if we borrowed his map?"

"Go for it. I never see him use it anyway."

"Thanks."

Holly now had two missions. Her first was to help uncover the town's mysterious disappearances. The second was to uncover the century old secrets lurking inside the McGuire mansion. She was determined not to fail at either task.

CHAPTER 3

Phyllis tossed back and forth in bed in the midst of a frightening dream. She saw herself in her kitchen preparing breakfast when all of a sudden the refrigerator opened all by itself. A milk carton floated out, and up in front of her face having on its one side a partial picture of one of the twins' faces. Next, canned goods and boxes of cereal started to float out of the cupboards, each having a piece of a picture on one side. The sight reminded her of a giant jigsaw puzzle. All the items started to rearrange themselves in front of her, each one going into its proper place till she could make out a solid image—a collage… a Picasso-like abstract that resembled in some ways the painting she was working on, but it was terribly different. It showed the twins with their arms extended out in front them, looking as if they were reaching out for help. There their dogs sat up on their hind legs, front paws raised, appearing as if they were begging for something. The scary image jolted Phyllis awake. She sat straight up in bed, feeling her heart pounding. She tried to convince herself that this dream and the changes to her painting were just figments of her imagination.

When Phyllis entered the kitchen, she was surprised to see Patrick and Holly already seated, eating cold cereal. "Next time you find me sleeping in, please wake me up so I can serve you something warm to eat."

In no time flat, she found herself in front of the stove preparing a fresh breakfast of sunny-side-up eggs and bacon. She smiled at them having a pale complexion and puffy eyes.

"Is anything wrong, dear?" said Patrick, leaning across the table, casting an expression of concern.

Phyllis shrugged her shoulders. "Everything's fine." She was eager to see them off so she could get back to her painting, but still fearful of what she may discover on the canvas.

"Well now, don't hesitate in letting us know if we can help with anything," said Patrick.

Holly and Patrick gave her a loving kiss before heading out of the house.

Phyllis entered her studio and slowly approached her painting with nerves about as steady as a house of cards ready to collapse at a moment's breath. As Phyllis neared the painting, she hid her face behind her hands. The instant she lowered them, her head made wide sweeping motions side to side. She couldn't believe her eyes. There were tears dripping from the twins' eyes! The corners of their mouths sagged open, appearing as if they were crying and calling out for someone. The dogs' ears drooped straight down, almost covering their eyes, left paws raised, reaching out, as if they were hurt, whimpering, calling for help.

That Afternoon

Holly waited at the corner of Roosevelt and Grand for Charlie to show up so they could go on their planned visit to Bellarouse's cornfield. It wasn't long before she spotted him coming around the corner.

"Sorry, for being late," said Charlie.

"It's OK. Well, which way to your aunt's house?"

He pointed down a dirt road that followed the riverbank. After traveling for about thirty minutes, they finally reached Bellaroure's house. Holly saw the front garden for the very first time, and was really amazed at what she saw. "Wow! Just look at that." There were plants and flowers arranged and trimmed to look like food items. Holly walked up to a cluster of plants that resembled a three-foot donut, planted with sugary white alyssum on the outside, and filled with clumps of purple lobelia at the center for a grape jelly look. Miniature hedges lined both sides of the walkway, trimmed and shaped to resemble loaves of bread.

Holly and Charlie hunched down and scurried from bush to bush, tree to tree, making their way around the side of the house, being careful not to make their presence known. Holly stopped and stared in disbelief at a deathly sight; the fifty holes Charlie described to her earlier, but they were all turned into small gravesites. The headstones spread across the lawn, all arranged in neat rows. On some of the newer plots had canning jars fill with freshly cut flowers. Holly knelt next to one of the graves. She could tell it was recently made, because it was covered with newly laid sod.

"I can't believe it. It's true. Everything you said was true," said Holly.

"Believe it or not," said Charlie, "What you are just witnessing is Marie's headless doll collection graveyard."

Holly glanced down and read the inscription on one of the headstones. It read, "Mary White, born December 2, 1999, died December 14, 1999, *WHAT A DOLL!*"

"I told you, Holly," said Charlie, "Marie's mind is spinning somewhere in outer space."

"I had doubts about what you told me before, but not anymore."

Dusk succumbed to night, and a blanket of stars rolled across the sky. Charlie and Holly crouched beneath a half way open window. They inhaled deeply, smelling freshly baked apple cinnamon pie. Charlie's stomach started to grumble. He leaned toward Holly and whispered into her ear, "She's always cooking… always."

Holly and Charlie peered through the window, catching a glimpse of the living room. The walls were decorated with blue ribbons and first-place trophies from every food contest imaginable: best dessert, fruit pie, Thanksgiving turkey, best-tasting chocolate Easter egg and many others.

The night's silence was suddenly shattered by the sound of Far Eastern music and the intermittent clanging of what sounded like brass cymbals. Bellarouse enter the room dressed as a belly dancer with her dog; a full-grown Saint Bernard. She was a large, round woman, with unnatural snow-white hair highlighted with streaks of purple. A large black mole, the size of a quarter, was visible, high on her right cheek. She smiled through a pink silk veil that draped low across her face. Her large legs were partially covered with a flowing blue silk skirt, speckled with gold glitter. She danced around her dog, rolling her hips, arching her back, and swaying her body from side to side, all the while making clanging sounds with her zills—brass finger cymbals—in her right hand.

Bellarouse suddenly stopped dancing and sashayed up to her dog. "Mitchell, my sugar pie honey bun. You know what I want… don't you?" she said, blowing him a kiss. Mitchell shook his head.

"Mitchell is her husband's name," said Charlie, "I wonder why she would be calling her dog by her husband's name?"

Inside the living room, Bellarouse continued to prod her dog on. "Come on. Open wide. Open those choppers for me."

He shook his head and clamped his jaws shut.

"You know I can't dance with just one pair of clickers. Give them to me. Give them to me now!"

"Marmalade butterscotch ice cream for you, baby," she said, whispering into his ear.

The dog's eyes suddenly stretched wide. His head nodded up and down. The sides of his muzzle flopped about in all directions, sending gobs of saliva dive-bombing onto the knotty pine floor.

Bellarouse smiled through her silk veil, nodding in unison with Mitchell. "Yes, yes. That's right! You know that's your favorite dessert, don't you?" She put her face close to his, dropped the silk veil from her face and gave him a big grin. "Open wide now. Come on. Come on. Open up. Open up."

The moment Mitchell dropped his mouth open, Bellarouse reached inside and removed his false teeth, then resumed her dancing, clanging her brass zills in one hand while snapping Mitchell's teeth in the other. She headed toward the doorway. "Getting your sweets now, you sugar pie honey dog."

Just outside the window, a small twig snapped beneath Holly's foot. The noise caught Mitchell's keen hearing. He headed over to the window, plopped his front legs onto the windowsill and looked out. Just then, Bellarouse re-entered the room carrying a gold platter with a domed top.

"Mitchell, what are you doing with your head stuck out the window like that?"

Mitchell caught sight of Charlie and Holly crouched beneath the window.

"Well, Mitchell? What's the matter with you? Is anything the matter? See anything boy?" she said, taking a few steps toward the window.

Mitchell focused his attention on the platter containing the mouthwatering sweets he was about to partake. Just the slightest thought of food caused his salivary glands to go into overdrive.

"Well Mitchell," Bellarouse repeated, "Do you see anything out there?"

Charlie glanced up at Mitchell and put his index finger to his lips, gesturing for him not to give away their presence.

Mitchell looked back at Bellarouse, shaking his head.

"Well, then, come to your better half," she said smiling, "Your dessert is starting to get soft."

Bellarouse knelt down and placed the serving

tray on the floor, then raised the domed top, revealing three large scoops of butterscotch ice cream. Mitchell raised his muzzle and exposed his pink gums, eyes focused on Bellarouse's lips.

"One…" said Bellarouse, starting the countdown. Mitchell lowered his head closer to the ice cream.

"Two…"

Mitchell moved his saliva-dripping mouth six inches above the treat.

"Three!"

The moment finally arrived and Mitchell dove in, inhaling one ball of ice cream at a time. After swallowing the last one, he shook his head back and forth.

"Mitchell, you giant hot dog, you," said Bellarouse, "Did you get brain freeze again?"

Mitchell pitifully nodded.

Bellarouse's daughter, Marie, stomped into the living room carrying six empty containers of strawberry yogurt. Her pitch black hair was highlighted with streaks of pink. She was wearing a black dress patterned with tiny red hearts with arrows pierced through. "Mother!" Marie shouted. A web of hair like veins spread across her white cheeks.

"Yes, honey chucks?"

"Don't call me honey chucks!" She gave her a mean look. "I wanted seven. There are only six… you promised seven containers of yogurt for bedtime!"

"But, cream puff, the store only had six left in your flavor."

"Don't call me cream puff!" She dropped to her knees and pounded her fists on the floor. "I don't care if you have to go to the North Pole and mix strawberries with ice by hand. I want one more strawberry yogurt, and I want it now!"

"Oh, my baby strawberry cheesecake. But too much sugar isn't good for your teeth, and besides, how am I going to get to the North Pole without any flying reindeer?"

"Don't call me cheesecake! If you can't figure out how to fly and get it, I'll… I'll turn into the most terrible monster in the world and make everyone serve me hand and foot!"

"Why, angel cake…"

"Don't call me angel cake! I'm not an angel!" she hollered, pounding the floor.

Just outside the window, Holly gazed at Charlie. "At least she's honest, saying she's not an angel. I think we've both heard enough complaining for one lifetime. That little brat!" Holly gazed toward Bellarouse's cornfield. "It's too dark to search her field tonight."

Charlie nodded. "We best be coming back another time when we can get an earlier start."

"Let's check out your uncle's shack instead," said Holly.

"You're not serious?"

"You said the place is deserted. Right? I'd just like to see if I could help find some clue that might shed some light on the reason why your Uncle Melvin disappeared."

"You must be pretty brave to venture there in the dead of night. You're not going to get spooked by Nightmare… are you?"

"Hey… you can be my bodyguard. Right?"

Charlie sighed. "Sure," he said, gazing down at his skimpy muscles. "OK, let's go check it out."

* * * * *

About twenty minutes later, they reached Melvin's cabin. Holly noticed that it was heavily splintered and cracked. Four log posts propped up the backside to keep it from sliding down the hill and into the river.

As Holly reached out to open the front door, she felt the tips of Charlie's shoes press against the back of her heels.

He gripped her shoulder. "Are you sure you want to go inside?"

Holly nodded, then slowly creaked the door open. The noise spooked an owl perched on an overhead branch. It took flight, screeching through the night sky.

Holly and Charlie stepped into the living room

and saw tattered curtains and a ripped sofa. Upon entering the kitchen, they saw paint peeling off the walls and cupboards. Charlie stood next to the dining table and placed his hand on a wobbly chair. If it weren't for the moonlight shining through the windows, it would be pitch-black inside.

Holly cringed her nose, smelling sour milk. "It really stinks in here," said Holly. "I think if we put a canary in here it would be singing the blues as its last performance, then drop dead for an encore."

Charlie nodded. "I totally agree."

Neither of them were able to escape the odor, but their curiosity kept them inching forward, hoping to discover some new clue.

Holly squinted through the shadows. "Do you think that wicked cat is somewhere in here?"

He shrugged his shoulders. "Never can tell. Could be anywhere. Even outside, perhaps enjoying a three course mouse dinner."

All of a sudden, they heard a hissing growl, followed by flaming yellow eyes glaring back down at them from the overhead cabinet shelf.

Before Holly or Charlie had the chance to react, the creature leaped into the air, landing on the table behind them.

"Nightmare," said Charlie, "I should have figured you'd be lurking about in some dark corner."

Melvin's cat, nightmare of nightmares, looked exactly like how Charlie described it to Holly before.

It even had a nasty looking "X" scar on its forehead.

The cat looked up at Holly with a twitching left eye, then started to purr the instant she stroked its back. His hairless tail whipped back and forth against her shirt, while his pink tongue kept licking her arm. "Oh Nightmare, you cuddly prowler of the night. Are you trying to make up for scaring the daylights out of us?" Holly chuckled. "His tongue feels ticklish, like wet sandpaper."

"Looks as if Nightmare has taken an instant liking to you. It's very unusual for that cat to make friends with anyone except my uncle Melvin. You must have a way with wild cats. Perhaps you might consider adopting Nightmare. What do you think?"

Holly grinned. "No insult intended for the cat, but every morning I'd wake up with him staring back at me from my pillow I would be thinking I was having double nightmares."

Charlie chuckled. "Yeah… I know what you mean."

Nightmare's eye continued to twitch. Charlie saw what looked like tears beading down the corner of his eyes. "I think Nightmare might be crying."

"Hope it wasn't anything I said. I wouldn't want to give him a worse nightmare than he already is."

Nightmare leaped onto the kitchen counter and knocked over a rusted half-gallon container, spilling white flour across the floor. Next, the cat leaped down and started to roll back and forth on top of it until he spread an even layer across the floor.

Charlie looked puzzled. "What's that cat up to?"

Holly pointed at the floor. "Look!"

Nightmare was scratching out letters in the flour with his right paw.

Charlie read out each letter as it appeared.

"D-A-N-G-E-R!"

Nightmare looked up at them and screeched.

Holly peered out the kitchen window. "He's warning us about something. But what?"

Nightmare scratched out more letters.

"R-U-N!"

When they didn't move, Nightmare leaped onto Charlie's back and screeched into his ear.

Charlie decided it was a good time to take the cat's advice and:

"R-U-N!"

He sprinted out the front door while trying to shake the cat off his back. Holly came up from behind and pulled him off.

Next, they ran flat out down the road. Glancing back over their shoulder, they caught a glimpse of two bodily forms in the distance that looked human, but were not, for they could see right through them. The glowing figures suddenly took aim at them with what looked like some kind of weapon.

Holly shouted, "Get down!"

They both flew flat on the grass. Glancing up, they saw two red laser beams flash directly overhead where they would have been standing.

Holly pointed down the embankment toward the Mississippi. "The river!"

They crawled through knee-high grass on their bellies, slid down a muddy slope, and into the river.

The surrounding countryside was completely silent as the river's current carried them downstream past Melvin's shack. Gone were the usual sounds of crickets and frogs. The Mississippi's cool water helped to calm their nerves as they floated down about half a mile. Minutes later, the welcoming sounds of the crickets and bullfrogs once again filled the air.

Holly pointed at a deer drinking from the shallow water. "It's probably safe to make it back to shore now. If there was anything unusual lurking around that deer it would be long gone."

Holly and Charlie dragged themselves out of the Mississippi, shivering and totally exhausted.

"This is a job for the sheriff," said Charlie.

"Problem is…who's going to believe us? What are we going to say? A cat used its paw to scratch out the word "danger" in flour, and a couple of alien looking creatures shot at us with ray guns?"

"I know where you're coming from, but what else to do?" said Charlie. "We nearly got shot at by something. Somebody!"

Holly took a deep breath. "Like I said, who's going to believe us? We need some real proof before going to the law."

"I guess you're right. Let's meet up again tomorrow."

Holly grinned. "Sounds good."

After giving each other a reassuring hug, they headed back to their homes.

CHAPTER 4

The moment Holly returned home she headed up the spiraling stairway and down the hallway. She suddenly stopped in front of Morgan's suite, thinking she heard something coming from just inside. She got down flat on the floor and peered through the narrow slit at the base of the door. Squinting into the darkness, she heard what sounded like the faint ticking of a grandfather clock with its pendulum swinging back and forth. The clock couldn't have been operating by itself for over a hundred years. There must be a force, something keeping it going, she thought. The ticking lulled Holly's mind back in time to a place where she dreamed of seeing Morgan sitting inside, looking out the window, with his two Great Danes sitting at his side.

Holly suddenly jolted her head back, feeling

a puff of air blow against her eye. At that same moment, she heard sniffing sounds coming from the other side of the door.

Next, she heard scratching noises, lasting for about fifteen seconds, followed by complete silence. Even the ticking had stopped. Holly placed her head flush with the floor. Peering into the darkness, she felt another puff of air. But this time, a white feather blew out through the crack and floated about two feet into the air. Before it reached the floor, another burst of air came seemingly out of nowhere and whisked it back up again, propelling it toward the stairs that once led to the twins' attic, but was now blocked off by the solid wall. When the feather reached the stairs, the air stopped and the feather floated down, settling on the third step up. Holly noticed that the stair tread the feather landed on was sitting crooked from the others. She ran her hand across its surface and felt it move. After getting a pocketknife from her room she placed the blade between the boards and was able lift it out of place. It moved easily, and she was able to remove it completely. Inside the cavity, covered with cobwebs, was a small metal box. Gently, carefully, she raised the lid. To her surprise and delight, she discovered an old skeleton key.

Just then, Holly was startled by the sound of her father's voice calling out to her from the base of the stairs.

"Holly!" said Patrick.

She looked down the stairs and gave her dad a sweet smile, "Yes, dad," she said, wondering if he could detect a guilty look on her face, as if she was up to something.

"Holly, are you all right? You've been awful quiet lately."

"Um.. I'm OK, Dad. Thanks for checking on me," she said, slipping the key into her side pocket. The moment Patrick disappeared into his study she quickly replaced the box and shoved the stair tread back in place.

I wonder where this key goes too? she thought. Holly peeped outside her bedroom and down the hallway. She could hear her parents having a conversation in the kitchen area. Now's my chance to try out this key. She tiptoed down the hallway to Morgan's suite, then slipped the key into its large padlock. It rotated a quarter turn, then froze. She sighed. Where, where else could this key possibly go too? She remembered that the only other room in the mansion that was locked and didn't have a key was the basement door. "Maybe… quite possibly…" she whispered to herself, quickly heading downstairs. The basement door was near the kitchen, but, fortunately, out of her parents' line of sight. She held her breath as she slipped the key into the lock and turned it, hoping it wouldn't make any noise. She felt a sudden rush when she heard it click to the open position. "Yes. Yes!" she whispered.

After retrieving her flashlight, she entered the basement. The steps leading down were old and rotten, creaking and bowing beneath her feet as she went down. The sound reminded her of the music she made during her first violin lesson. She stopped for a moment, then looked back upstairs toward the door, hoping that her parents didn't hear the creaking sounds. After reaching the bottom, she grabbed an old curtain rod and started to slice away the cobwebs that draped before her. On the west wall, she saw sagging wood plank shelves filled with canning jars. One glass container had a crinkled label attached with the handwritten words, Apricot Preserves.

Squinting through the shadows, Holly caught sight of a solid wall of wooden apple crates stacked all the way up to the ceiling. She beamed her flashlight between them and noticed that they were all wired together. How odd. Why would anyone go to so much trouble? What seemed even more peculiar was that someone had attached wheels to the bottom of the crates. She reached out and grabbed one of the cartons and was able to pull the entire wall of crates back like a giant door. "Yes!" she whispered excitedly. On the opposite side, she discovered another hidden door. Upon opening it, she discovered a secret stone stairway that spiraled up as it ascended. Looking about, she saw rotting pieces of cloth tapestry clinging to the stone walls.

Something immediately caught her attention on the fourth step up. It was a large, tightly wadded ball of newspaper. She picked it up and rolled it in her palms, observing it from all sides. She carefully unfolded the edges until she was able to see the entire page. Her heart skipped a beat as she read the front headlines. In large bold letters it read, **"Morgan McGuire's Twins Mysteriously Disappear."** The small print to the story was too faded to read, however, she was able to make out the image of Morgan holding two photos of his twin daughters in front of him. Sitting on either side of him were his two Great Danes. They appeared to be skinny and looked very unhappy. One might even think, by looking at their faces, that they were very angry about something.

All of a sudden, a numbing wind whirled down the passageway carrying with it the sound of a pipe organ's funeral note stuck on it lowest pitch. Holly bravely proceeded up the steps. She felt the wind blow against her shirt and pants as she continued upward. Her hair floated back, whisked first to one side, then the other. A cobweb covered with dust suddenly took flight and landed squarely across her face. She raised her hand up and quickly wiped it off, then sneezed and twitched her nose to get rid of the dust.

The stairs seemed to never end as they twisted

upward. She came to a landing and stood before a splintered oak door with the image of two large dogs carved into its surface. The cast-iron doorknob was in the shape of a bulldog's head. Holly was fairly certain on the other side of the door was the back entrance to Morgan's master suite. The instant she gripped the doorknob, the wind ceased, leaving in its place an eerie silence. She reached into her shorts and tried the skeleton key, but couldn't get it to open the door. She turned and refocused her attention toward the top of the stairs. The attic might be up there, she thought. Holly hadn't taken more than two steps up when the wind started to blow again, but this time from the opposite direction, against her back, as if something or someone wanted her to continue up the stairs. To her surprise, with each step forward the wind felt warmer and more inviting.

As Holly made the last turn up the passageway, her eyes stretched wide with excitement seeing another door at the very top. It appeared to be made of stained oak. Stepping closer, she noticed something very disturbing about it. The elegantly carved images of flowers and gardens on the door's surface were damaged, as if someone had taken a hatchet to the surface. Strips of wood had been chopped out and lay rotting at her feet. She reached out for the doorknob and turned it slowly, but it was locked. She tried the skeleton key, and to her surprise, and delight, it worked! Her flashlight suddenly dimmed. She tapped it against her side to get it working, but it went out completely. Taking a deep breath, she reached out and creaked the door open, then leaned forward and squinted inside a room deep in shadow.

CHAPTER 5

The moment Holly entered the room, the clouds parted and moonlight beamed through the window, exposing its shadowy secrets. Her attention was drawn to a big lump covered with a moth eaten blanket on the bottom bunk bed.

"I just have to know what's under there," she thought. Her feet inched closer to the bed. "Okay… On the count of three." She took a deep breath and started counting, "One… two… three!" then reached out and flung back the cover. Her eyes stretched wide in shock seeing a skeleton lying on the mattress with its head resting upon a pillow of feathers. They weren't just ordinary feathers. They were the exact same size, shape and color as the feather she saw back inside the mansion that helped guide her to the key that unlocked the basement and attic door.

Holly heard the whistle from an approaching steamboat. That same instant, the lantern on the windowsill sparked a small flame within its glass casing that grew brighter by the second.

Holly felt her heart start to beat fast, catching sight of a ghostly image peering down at her from the top bunk. Another bodily form appeared to float up from the lower bed. Holly was fairly certain they were the same two girls she had seen just prior to her falling out the window that one night.

The twins had matching yellow ribbons tied to their chestnut hair, and were dressed in red-and-white plaid dresses with shoulder sleeves puffed out around the edges. A moment later, they disappeared before her eyes. Where…? Where did they go? Holly spun in a circle. The door slammed shut behind her, and one of the twins appeared directly in front of it, blocking her way out. Are they trying to trap me in here? Holly was frantic. She peered back over her shoulder and saw the second twin standing in front of the lantern by the window. Holly took a deep breath. My only two ways out are blocked. She peered right through the twin by the window and saw the flame of the lantern glow brightly behind her. An icy chill passed through her body. "What was that?" she said, seeing a white mist float out in front of her. She blinked to clear her vision. Both twins stood by the window and stared back at her with large doll-like eyes. A sudden gust of wind blew through the window, and their ghostly bodies rippled like flapping white sheets.

Holly retreated toward the door, not knowing for sure if they were friendly or not. With each step back, they took one step forward. Holly backed up against the door, then reached behind her and grasped the knob. Right then she had to make a quick decision: confront the ghosts, or run! After a moment's hesitation, she decided to take a brazen step forward. "I… I'm Holly. I'm here to try and help you."

They continued to stare at her in silence with wide-stretched eyes. Holly was about to make a quick exit, when she noticed faint smiles suddenly blossom upon their faces that kept getting bigger until their expressions flamed with warmth.

"I'm Stephanie, Miss Holly," said the twin on the left.

"I'm Agatha," said the other.

Their ghostly hands stretched out to her.

Holly reached out to shake their hands but felt nothing to hold onto.

"Miss Holly, we know who you are. We're glad you're here," said Stephanie, "they didn't mean to do us harm."

"Yes, yes, they didn't mean to do us harm, you see, you see," said Agatha, casting a sad expression, with her eyebrows sinking low.

Their voices seemed to resonate like an eerie echo. Holly saw tears swell up, then roll down the sides of their cheeks.

"Who didn't mean to do you harm?" she asked, looking puzzled.

Agatha raised her arm and pressed her palm over her heart. "Papa was sick. Really, he was… he was," she said. "He was the one who told them to do it."

Holly stepped closer. "Told who to do what?"

Stephanie's eyes narrowed. "Miss Holly, it was Papa, you know." She moved closer, staring into her face. "You see, Papa thought our dogs, Spitz and Mitra, stole away our love."

"The Great Danes?" she said with raised eyebrows.

They nodded, staring at her stone-faced.

"Really, Miss Holly, Papa became insanely jealous. He turned them against us."

"Yes, yes… against us," said Agatha, appearing very sad. She glanced first at her sister, then at Holly.

"Miss Holly, Papa put our picture in front of the dogs when they ate. When we looked a moment later, we knew Papa had taken their food away. It was gone."

"Yes… gone, gone," said Agatha.

"Later, the dogs began to growl at our picture, Miss Holly. Later they began to growl at us. The dogs became skinnier and thinner."

Agatha stepped up to Holly, eyes stretched wide, "Yes, skinny, skinny."

"You mean the dogs learned to associate you

two with someone taking away their food?"

Stephanie nodded. "Papa was sick."

"He had ways… ways," said Agatha.

"Did you raise the dogs from puppies?"

"Yes, Miss Holly. They were special gifts to us. Close friends of Papa brought them here all the way from Germany. Papa trained them to be kind."

Holly could see tears drip down their faces.

Stephanie reached out and placed her hand upon Holly's shoulder, "The dogs became mean—hunters again!"

Holly saw fear in their eyes.

"Our dogs, Mitra and Spitz are still here… are here," said Agatha, gazing toward the door leading down the hallway.

"You mean in the room below us?"

They both nodded.

Okay, now this is getting a little scary, she thought. Holly took a deep breath and stared blankly ahead in deep thought for a moment, then suddenly turned and faced the twins with a smile. "Yes, it might possibly work," she said. Looking about the room, she spied three photographs hanging on the wall taken of the twins with their Great Danes at a time when they were happy and playing together.

"Can I borrow these three pictures?"

They nodded, but appeared a little confused.

"Yes, but what for…what for?" said Agatha. She took one of the silver framed photos off the wall and placed it firmly over her heart.

"I can't explain everything at this moment. I have an idea…a crazy one, but it's worth a try. Do you have a way of unlocking the back door to the master suite… the one off the stone stairway?"

The twins looked at each other for a couple seconds, then shifted their attention back to Holly and nodded.

"Great," she said, snapping her fingers. She gathered all the pictures into her arms. "I'll be back. Have the door to the master suite unlocked. I'll be there in about twenty minutes."

Agatha reached out toward Holly. "Be careful. Please, you promise… promise?"

Holly looked back, nodding. "Yes, you can be sure of that. I'll be careful. Don't worry."

Tears of new-found hope welled up in the corners of Stephanie and Agatha's eyes as they watched Holly head out the door.

CHAPTER 6

Holly headed across the foyer and into the dining room. Just like clockwork, about five minutes into dinnertime, Phyllis and Patrick became actively engaged in chatting about the latest news events. While they were busy talking, Holly seated herself at the table and started sneaking small portions of meatloaf off her plate and into a plastic bag on her lap.

Phyllis gazed over at Holly's plate. "You sure have a hearty appetite this evening."

Holly tilted her head to one side and grinned. "You outdid yourself. This meatloaf looks great!"

Phyllis leaned forward and smiled. "I hope it tastes great too."

Holly gave her a thumbs-up sign of approval. "All your cooking is wonderful, Mom."

As soon as her parents resumed their conversation, she slipped the bag of meatloaf underneath her sweater. The meat felt warm against her skin.

"Mom… I'm stuffed, literally." Holly gazed nervously across the table. "Can I please be excused?"

Phyllis smiled. "Of course."

Holly made her way out of the dining room, being careful to keep her bulging side containing the bag of food out of her parents' line of vision.

Next, she reentered the basement and headed up the secret stone passageway. A moment later, she found herself in front of the back door to Morgan's master suite. Taking a deep breath, she grasped the iron doorknob. "Yes! Yes!" she whispered to herself, hearing the door click open. She felt happy, but at the same time somewhat fearful of what she might find lurking about inside the suite.

Holly creaked the door open, exposing the room to its first breath of fresh air in over a hundred years. The moment she poked her head inside, she noticed a strange, musty, stagnant odor, like one might find in a sealed tomb.

She panned her flashlight around the room, then suddenly froze, seeing what appeared to be the skeletons of two large dogs sitting on either side of a large leather chair. The frightful sight made her feel very uneasy, but she remained firm and unmovable, focusing all her thoughts on helping her two friends upstairs. She was determined not to let them down, no matter what she came up against.

The dogs and chair faced the draped windows. If the curtains were drawn back, there would be a beautiful view overlooking the Mississippi river. Holly emptied her bag of meatloaf onto the floor, then placed one of the pictures of the twins next to the food. She whistled and called out the dogs' names, "Spitz! Mitra!"

Holly was shocked to see the dogs' heads start to creak and turn back. Suddenly, without warning, they sprung onto their feet and charged right at her. She fled the room, slamming the door tightly shut behind her. She placed her ear to the door, and heard what sounded like chewing and chomping sounds. Two minutes later, the noise stopped, and was followed by complete silence.

Holly creaked the door open, just enough to peep inside. She took notice that the dogs were back on either side of the leather chair and faced the curtains, but something seemingly unbelievable happened to them. There appeared to be new skin, hair, and flesh halfway up their bodies, starting from the tip of their tail to their midsection.

Looking down, she noticed that the twins' photo had been knocked face down on the floor. She picked up the frame and discovered the glass had been shattered into a hundred pieces. Holly was deeply disturbed at the sight of the picture, but the miraculous improvement in the dogs' appearance made her think she might be onto something.

She raised her finger to her chin and wondered if there might be a chance to get the dogs to connect the food offering with the picture of the twins. She hoped with all her heart she could help restore the love that once existed between the children and the dogs.

Minutes later, she reappeared in the mansion's kitchen. After checking to make sure the coast was clear, she raided the refrigerator. She packed two more bags with various food items, including canned salmon, tuna, and even vanilla ice cream.

She hurried back to the basement and retraced her steps up the stairway to Morgan's suite, then slowly opened the door and placed the second of three pictures she borrowed from the twins inside the room, together with some salmon and ice cream. The instant she whistled, the dogs charged back at her with their glowing eyes and snapping teeth. Without a second to lose Holly slammed the door shut behind her. The next moment, she heard gobbling noises. As soon it became silent, she peeked inside. To her surprise, she discovered the dogs' skeletons almost entirely covered with flesh, from their tails up to their necks. She looked down at the second picture of the twins and noticed that the frame had been knocked over, but it had landed face up. The glass was cracked slightly, but not violently broken as the one before it.

She decided to repeat the same procedure one more time. She placed the third serving of food with a little leftover ice cream for good luck, together with the last picture inside the room. When the chewing sounds stopped and there was complete silence, she checked to see the results.

The dogs appeared to be resting once again on either side of the leather chair, but this time with their bodies appeared to be whole and healthy. Even their coats looked shiny.

A smile broke upon Holly's face as she gazed down at the third picture. It was still standing, There appeared to be saliva dripping down the glass, as if the dogs had been licking it. The dogs remained on either side of the chair and showed no signs of aggression. She exited the room, making sure the door was securely shut, before heading up the stairway.

CHAPTER 7

When Holly reentered the attic, she saw Agatha and Stephanie standing by the window, staring back at her with blank expressions.

Holly's face broke out into a big smile. "I want you to come with me," she said, gesturing with her hands for them to follow her.

Agatha tilted her head to one side and gave her a curious look. "But where… where?"

"Downstairs… inside the master suite… where your dogs are."

Holly's words had the twins terrified. They shook their heads and backed up against the wall.

Stephanie took a deep breath and a short step forward, "But, Miss Holly, they hate us, really."

She waved them forward. "Please… come. Trust me. I believe they've changed. I believe they wanted to love you all along, and now have every reason too."

The twins looked at each other in silence with blank expressions, then glanced back at Holly.

I wonder if they will trust me enough so that they can meet the dogs face to face, she thought.

After some hesitation, the twins' expressions grew hopeful.

Holly kept waving them forward. "Come… trust me… let's go."

They slowly followed Holly's lead downstairs and into the master suite. When their dogs, Spitz and Mitra, first saw the twins, they stared at them squinty-eyed, and showed their teeth. They could hear deep-throated growls. The twins clasped their hands tightly together for fear of what might happen next. The dogs headed across the room, then suddenly stopped and stared down at the pictures on the floor: the shattered frame, the frame knocked down, and lastly, the one still standing. The dogs' teeth were no longer visible and their stubby tails began to twitch back and forth. Instead of pouncing on the twins, they approached in puppyish leaps and bounds, and began to lick their faces. Holly felt so happy for them.

The twins looked back at Holly with glowing faces and happy smiles.

"How can we ever repay you?" said Agatha.

Holly thought for a moment, then spoke up.

"Well, there is just one thing. I believe that the town of Kingston could be in some kind of danger."

"From what?" asked Agatha, casting a worried expression.

"Well… this may be hard to grasp, but…"

"Yes, Miss Holly, tell us?" said Stephanie.

"Foreign beings. Possibly from another galaxy!"

The twins raised their hands to their mouths and started to giggle.

"Aliens from the stars, Miss Holly?" said Stephanie.

Holly nodded, with a very serious look about her. Their giggling and smiles stopped, and were replaced with expressions of concern. The twins looked at each other for a moment in silence, then stared back into Holly's eyes.

"Yes, we will help you. We will… we will," said Agatha, with a firm nod.

"Yes, Miss Holly, really, just tell us what we must do," said Stephanie.

Holly confided everything she knew about the aliens, and how they could possibly use their invisible powers spy out Bellarouse's house, and gather important information to help her. She said that they must be extra careful, as she didn't know if their invisible nature would work against the aliens. Moments later, the twins and their dogs disappeared before Holly's eyes, leaving her alone in the room to ponder her next plan of action.

* * * * *

Holly reappeared inside the front entranceway to the mansion, then headed across the foyer. She heard her parents talking within the art studio, and took a peek inside. She saw them standing side-by-side staring in silence at the painting of the twins and their dogs. Holly walked up to them and peered around her dad's shoulder. "What's going on?"

"How? How can it be?" said Phyllis. The painting of Agatha and Stephanie showed them having vibrant, happy faces. Pink hues blossomed like roses upon their cheeks. Even Mitra and Spitz appeared full-bodied, super healthy, and smiling. They had pointy ears, sparkling eyes, and their coats appeared to glow from the reflection of sunlight off the canvas.

Patrick leaned forward for a closer look, "What on Earth did you do to the dogs' faces, Honey?"

Phyllis gazed back with a puzzled look. "Patrick, whatever do you mean?"

Holly took a quick look. Her nose almost touched the painting as she peered at the dogs, "Oh… my… gosh," she said, looking very surprised.

Holly stepped aside, as Phyllis moved in front, placing her magnifying glass over the dogs' faces. "I can't believe it. It can't be," she said, seeing what looked like small pieces of food stuck around the dogs' lips. "Patrick, honey, there appears to be bits of meat loaf and vanilla ice cream on the dogs' faces. Exactly the same foods I served up for supper tonight. How is that possible? Is this some sort of joke?"

The three of them exchanged glances for a moment, then stared back at the painting, looking very puzzled.

Phyllis slowly looked over at Holly, squinty eyed. "Holly darling, would you know anything about how this might have happened?"

"Now Mom…what are you thinking? Could you imagine in your wildest dreams me sneaking bits of food off my dinner plate, and then figure out a way to get it on the dogs' faces?"

"Well, I guess that would be a bit hard to imagine. After all, you were a hearty eater tonight and didn't leave anything on your plate."

Moments later, Holly phoned Charlie and told him everything that had happened, but he kept interrupting, telling her she must have been dreaming.

CHAPTER 8

Holly met up with Charlie for their planned visit to Bellarouse's cornfield.

"Sorry I'm late," said Holly.

Charlie glanced at her as they headed down the dirt road. "I have an interesting story for you," he said.

Holly gave him her full attention. "Okay… let's hear it."

"I overheard my mom talking with Annabel Drusky, Bellarouse's next door neighbor. She said Annabel has been calling everyone in town!" Charlie stood in front of Holly for a moment and stared into her eyes. "She sounded freaked!"

"About what?"

"She was crying because her son, Albert. He

somehow disappeared after he chased his pet pig, Button Rouge, into Bellarouse's cornfield."

Holly's eyes widened. "Button Rouge… Bellarouse… cornfield?"

"Yeah, Annabel told my mom her son was out back playing baseball with his buds, Mitch and Shane, when they noticed Button Rouge having an all-you-can-eat pig-buffet in Bellarouse's vegetable patch. Albert climbed over the fence and chased his pig into the field."

"And?" said Holly, breathing deeper as they walked faster down the dirt road leading to Bellarouse's house and farm.

"Shane told Annabel that he and Mitch had called out over and over again for Albert, but he never came back out. Mitch said they saw two beams of red light flash out from the midst of the field. At that same instant they heard a scream followed by a loud squeal. They said the scream sounded like Albert!"

She looked at Charlie with wide stretched eyes. "Albert? Oh No! Poor kid! Could we pay the Drusky's a short visit on the way to Bellarouse's field? Is that possible?"

"Why would you want to stop there?"

"I would love to help find out what happened to their son and get him back. Perhaps we could pick up on something that was overlooked."

"Well…Albert's mom and family are still pretty

shook up right now, but maybe… a short visit wouldn't hurt."

* * * * *

On their way to Druskey's farm, Charlie stopped by a white picket fence to Dr. Spencer's residence, a newly renovated three story, white farmhouse complete with a chicken coop on one side and horse training arena on the other.

"The family that lives in that house just recently moved there from the big city," said Charlie, "The kids are clueless about farm life. They only know the basics, like cats, dogs, and zoo animals."

Holly gave him a puzzled look. "Zoo animals?"

"Dr. Spencer is a veterinarian. His specialty is exotic zoo animals."

"In Kingston? I didn't know they had a zoo here?"

"It just happens that the city council voted to build one. It will be opening soon! Aren't you excited?"

"Uh…Yeah. I couldn't think of a happier place to spend my day!" She reached into her back pocket and pulled out their map. "Can you show me on your dad's map where the zoo is located?"

Charlie pointed to a seventy-acre plot of land on the north side of town. "It doesn't show on this map because the zoo is so new and this map is old.

But the zoo and a new park are located right here. I believe the grand opening will take place in about a week from now. The land was donated to the city by my Uncle Waldo."

Holly gave Charlie a curious look. "Where is your Uncle Waldo?"

"That's a good question. He's always traveling, so it's hard to know exactly where Uncle Waldo is most of the time. It's almost like playing a game, like, trying to figure out where he is."

As they approached Dr. Spencer's home, his five-year old daughter, Jenny Spencer, ran around the side of the house ringing a bell in her hand while chasing a red rooster. Charlie called Jenny over to the front gate. "Jenny, what are you up to?"

"Three foot six," she said, leaning upwards, balancing herself on the tips of her toes. Charlie and Holly tried to keep a straight face.

"No, I mean, what are you doing?" said Charlie.

Jenny put her hand to her mouth and giggled. "My dad said in order to get the chicken ready for dinner I had to go outside and ring its neck."

Charlie chuckled. "You're a total jokester. I didn't see you as usual out playing basketball at the Boys and Girls Club last week."

Jenny coughed and sniffled. "I was sick and my nose was double dribbling."

Holly grinned. "That's foul."

Jenny looked back at the rooster. "See yah," she

said, waving goodbye, "I've got to get this chicken ready for dinner." That being said, she started to chase the rooster while ringing her bell.

Charlie spotted Patricia Burkhart step out onto the front porch of the Spencer residence. She tipped her white cowboy hat at Charlie and Holly.

Charlie waved back, then turned toward Holly. "That's Jenny's cousin visiting from Montana. My brother Kent has a crush on her."

"She looks kind of hip country. Maybe she can give the family a few pointers on preparing chicken."

Charlie nodded. "Right. Country fresh chicken with a nice ring to it."

* * * * *

Holly and Charlie continued down the road for about another mile before they reached the Drusky's farm, located on the east side of Bellarouse's property. The main house was shaped like a giant red barn, and had white trim around the windows and doors. A stiff wind suddenly kicked up. Holly saw the propeller of the seventy-five-foot-high windmill turn and pump well water into a large oval shaped pond located about eighty feet away from the house. The pond water was surrounded by bare dirt, with the exception of a giant willow tree growing by the water's edge. Its droopy foliage draped fifteen feet out over the pond. The tips of several branches dipped into the water, rippling a reflection of tree and sky.

A hundred feet from the pond was a large barn, having the unmistakable aroma of pigs, over sixty of them to be exact, Button Rouge being the odd lot. Their distinctive smell spread through every crack of the building. Even from sixty feet away, one could easily detect the sweet aroma…well, sweet from a pig's sense of smell.

Inside the barn were five rows of connected pens, each six by eight feet in diameter. Button Rouge had a special enclosure all to himself by the barn door. A hayloft ran along the east side of the barn. Piggish activity abounded—eating, drinking, playing chase, and, of course making snorting and squealing noises, which could be heard all the way out to the road.

"Well," said Charlie as they headed toward the front door to the Druskys' house, taking in the sights, sounds, and smells. "Do you still want to see Button Rouge?"

"You bet I do."

The wind suddenly shifted, carrying with it the smell from the barn. Holly stopped and faced Charlie. "Is there anything else you can tell me about the Druskys that might be helpful in finding more clues before talking to them?"

"Well… Albert's dad, Frank Drusky, is an airfreight delivery pilot turned part-time pig farmer. He works out of Brookdale Airport— that's about three miles east of here. He also used to work as a fulltime weatherman for "KDZ" TV station out of Jackson. He always had his head in the clouds." Charlie gazed toward the sky, then back toward the farm. "Now he's down here..." He shifted his attention toward the barn, "Raising pigs."

"Do the Druskys and Bellarouse get along?"

"Not at all. They're always at each other's throat, mostly because their pigs can't stay clear of her vegetable garden."

"Sounds like Bellarouse really has it out for them."

Charlie reached out and buzzed the doorbell.

Annabel rushed to the front door. "Have you seen... seen my Albert?" she said nervously, eyes darting back and forth between the two of them.

Before they could answer, Frank Drusky stepped up to his wife and placed his arm around her shoulder. Holly looked up and noticed he was wearing a pilot's hat with a shiny brass-winged emblem pinned to the front.

"Have you seen our son?" he said in a deep voice.

"I've been doing my best to keep a lookout for him," said Charlie. "This is my friend, Holly. She recently moved to Kingston, and is really eager to help join the search to find your son."

Albert's sister, Meagan, popped her head out

from her upstairs bedroom. "Mom. Who is it? Did they find Albert?"

Annabel looked upstairs. "Sorry, not yet. We have some guests now who are going to help in the search."

Holly stepped forward. "Could we see Button Rouge? I know it sounds weird, but it may help us in discovering a new clue to your son's whereabouts."

Annabel and Frank looked at each other in a moment in silence, then looked back and nodded. "Well, okay, but… um… I don't know what good it will do," said Frank, sighing.

Annabel spoke up, "Button Rouge is in his pen, in the barn, doing time for being a bad piggy." She looked up at Frank with a puzzled expression. "I just can't understand why Button all of a sudden has taken a liking to be gettin' in the house."

Holly and Charlie stared at each other for a moment, then looked back at Annabel.

"Now there's one more thing," said Annabel, "Button Rouge can act a bit aggressive when Bernie's Ham-It-Up truck comes to take the other pigs."

"Ham-It-Up?" said Holly, looking confused.

"The pig buyer," said Frank. "He's due to be comin' around in the not too distant future."

Annabel pointed at Charlie and Holly. "Now you two be careful, or you might get nipped." That being said, she suddenly broke out into tears.

Frank put his arm around her. "Try to keep

your spirits up. We'll find him. I'm taking the truck into town now. Lance and I are going to search north of here."

Annabel waved Frank and Lance off as Holly and Charlie headed toward the barn.

CHAPTER 9

The moment Charlie and Holly entered Drusky's barn, Button Rouge start to snort and squeal like crazy to get their attention.

Holly stepped up to his pen and looked down, "Button, do you know where Albert is?"

Charlie chuckled. "Do you think you're taking to Button Einstein?"

Holly gestured with her hand for Charlie to keep quiet. "Do you know where Albert is?" she said, staring down into Button's beady eyes.

Button looked up and nodded.

Holly smiled at Charlie. "I think he can lead us to Albert. "I think we should let him out and try to follow."

Charlie looked down at Button. "Just what if he decides to go into the vegetable patch again?" he said, gazing toward the open barn door. "Are you prepared to chase him into the cornfield… just in case?"

Holly pointed at the tears rolling down Button's face. "Look at him. Let him try. OK?"

Charlie sighed. "Well, don't say I didn't warn you."

As soon as Holly unlatched the pen, Button took off running straight toward the house. Holly raced right behind, but couldn't keep up.

"Oh, no! No!" said Holly, watching Button take a flying leap through the back screen door.

After Holly made formal apologies to Annabel for everything that had happened, Charlie helped her get Button back into his pen.

As Holly and Charlie continued down the dirt road toward Bellarouse's cornfield, they heard a vehicle approach from behind. Looking back, they saw a police car slowly heading their way.

"It's Sheriff Gary," said Charlie.

The sheriff stopped his car beside them.

"Hey…any of you come across any signs of Albert?" said the sheriff, gazing out the car window.

Charlie spoke up, "I'm sorry Sheriff Gary, no signs of him yet."

Sheriff Gary looked over his shoulder toward the backseat. "I'm here with Sergeant Rex, trying to sniff out more clues that might have been overlooked inside Bellarouse's cornfield."

Holly whispered to Charlie with a puzzled

expression on her face. "Sergeant Rex? Sniff out clues? I don't see anyone else in the car… do you?"

Charlie and Sheriff Gary smiled at each other. They knew something Holly didn't.

Out of sheer curiosity, she stepped up to the sheriff's car and peered in through the back window. All she could see was a large lump under a brown blanket spread across the seat. Sheriff Gary grinned. All of a sudden the blanket seemed to come alive, and flew up toward the ceiling. Holly jumped back and stumbled to the ground.

A large basset hound with big droopy ears leaped halfway out the side window and stared down at her with bloodshot eyes. Its head and tail teeter-tottered over the edge. Holly feared that at any moment the hound dog might slip out the window and land right on top of her.

Sheriff Gary looked out the side window at Holly. "Sorry about that, Miss," he said with a chuckle, watching her get back up.

"Sergeant Rex can be quite a stealthy dog," Charlie remarked.

Holly brushed dirt off her pants. "Yeah… he's also great at going undercover to find a good nap, don't you think?" Holly replied.

"That's Rex's top security blanket," said Sheriff Gary. "Very protective of it, he is."

Holly grinned. "I bet he hates dog-nappers. Except when it comes to himself, of course."

Sheriff Gary squinted at Holly. "Huh?" he said, not sure if she was insulting his best friend or not. "Remember, Rex here never totally sleeps. He's always at least partly on duty, twenty-four/seven, even if it's only his nose working. Anyway, I'm going to have him sniff out Bellarouse's cornfield now and retrace Albert's tracks. Now the two you keep safe." He left the pair on the side of the road, and continued toward the Bellarouse's farm."

Holly squinted through the dust as the sheriff drove off. "I think it's important we see what happens when Sheriff Gary confronts Bellarouse and tries to convince her to have another look-around her farm."

"Right," said Charlie, "Let's go."

Minutes Later

Holly and Charlie arrived just in time to see the sheriff head up Bellarouse's front steps. They hid behind a nearby hedge and kept a watchful eye on what was happening.

Before the sheriff had the chance to knock on the door, Bellarouse suddenly swung it open in front of him. "Yes… Sheriff… Gary?" said Bellarouse, squinting at him from behind the screen door. Sheriff Gary couldn't help but notice the large rolling pin in her right hand.

"Can I be helping you with somethin'?" she

said in a deep womanly voice.

"Ma'am, I… uh… have reason to believe that the neighbors' boy, Albert, may still be somewhere abouts nearby. I… uh… need to check your field again—with my partner, Sergeant Rex. Any objections?"

"Albert… corn? He hates corn," she said stepping out onto the front porch. "Hah…I know for a sure fact that boy hates corn. Is this search you be askin' some kind of bad recipe?" She gave him a sharp slap on the side of his shoulder.

"Huh, not at all, ma'am," he replied with a straight face. He tried not to show any sign of pain left from the sting she left on his arm. "If you want, I… ah… can come back with a search warrant…" he said, with his eyes narrowing.

Bellarouse peered around his shoulder. "Who… who is this Sergeant Rex you have with you? I don't see no one."

Sheriff Gary looked back toward his patrol car and whistled. Rex jumped up from under his blanket and popped his head out the back window. Bellarouse chuckled seeing part of the dog's blanket hanging over the side of his head.

"That's a pretty hot bojangle pooch you have there, Mr. Sheriff," she said. Her sneer suddenly changed into a wide grin. "Why, of course you can do some searchin'. You and that four-legged cadet of yours just go right ahead into my field and have one good corn lookin' time."

"Huh, thanks for your cooperation, man, I mean, ma'am."

Charlie peered over at Holly from behind the hedge. "I can't believe Bellarouse would let anyone onto her property without a fight."

Holly nodded. "I was a little worried when I saw that oversize rolling pin in her fist."

They watched Sheriff Gary and his dog head out toward the cornfield. About twenty feet away from the field, Rex suddenly stopped and raised his nose. He sniffed repeatedly, then let out a long drawn-out howl. Holly and Charlie watched Rex take off running into the cornfield with the Sheriff following close behind.

Minutes felt like hours. Charlie and Holly patiently remained crouched behind the hedge wishing that Sheriff Gary, Rex and Albert would come out all together, safe and sound.

Suddenly, Sergeant Rex burst out of the cornfield all by himself and ran like a scared rabbit out across the field. He made a beeline right for the police car, then took a giant leap inside. He sat up on the driver's seat and put his paws onto the steering wheel.

Holly watched Rex rock the steering wheel back and forth and honk the horn over and over again. "What's going on?"

Charlie blinked, not believing what he

was seeing before his eyes. "Wow! This can't be happening."

Holly motioned for Charlie to look through an opening in the hedge. He saw Bellarouse stare out her second story window with a big smile on her face watching Rex race back toward town with his tail tucked between his legs.

Holly gazed back toward the cornfield. "Now, where's Sheriff Gary?"

"One thing's for sure… he's not out there chuckin' corn," said Charlie, "We need to get help."

"Wait, who are we going to get? We just saw Sheriff Gary disappear and his dog run for his life. Let's check out the perimeter of the field to see if we can find the sheriff."

Charlie grabbed her arm and held her back. "No, that's way too dangerous."

"Hey, if we don't help out…"

"Let's lay low here for awhile and see if Bellarouse makes another move."

Holly nodded. "OK."

CHAPTER 10

Holly peered out from behind the bushes and saw Bellarouse slip out the back door of her house and head toward her cornfield. "There! There she goes!" she said.

Bellarouse stopped just short of the field, then turned and looked back toward the house.

Holly knelt lower behind the hedge and whispered into Charlie's ear, "Do you think she saw us?"

"Nope, from what I know about her, if that was the case, she'd be all over us by now."

Bellarouse reached out and parted the stalks of corn before her, then disappeared inside. Moments later, she reached the inner four-hundred-foot burnt circle of the cornfield. The entire area was void of any signs of plant or animal life. There wasn't even a solitary weed, insect or rodent to be seen anywhere. The cornstalks around the entire inner circle were scorched black. A stiff breeze suddenly kicked up and started to sway the cornstalks from side to side. Bellarouse reached into her apron pocket and removed a six-inch crystal. It was no ordinary mineral, for it possessed the clarity of the finest diamond, and was composed of a compound harder that any substance known on earth. The instant she raised the crystal up in front of her, beams of purple light shot forth, exposing a flying saucer nearly the same size as the inner diameter of the burnt circle.

The alien ship was translucent, like the skin of a giant bubble. Bellarouse gazed right through it, and could see the cornstalks on the opposite side of the field—only they looked blurred. A boarding ramp suddenly lowered in front of her. White sparks, like static electricity, buzzed around the edges of her shoes as she made her way up the ramp. She headed down a six-foot-wide corridor. The floor and walls appeared as opaque glass. A narrow channel ran down the center floor of the seventy-foot-long hallway, filled with a bluish liquid that sparked hair-like strands of electricity. As Bellarouse stepped forward, she heard faint popping and buzzing sounds about her feet. Continuing on, she gazed up through a two-foot-wide opening in the ceiling that ran down the entire length of the hallway. Her eyes stretched wide in awe seeing black space magnified millions of times. Shooting stars, planets, and glistening white clusters of far-away galaxies lay visible before her eyes.

At the end of the corridor, she made her way up three glass steps that led to a domed room a hundred feet in diameter, the apex being thirty feet high. It was made of seamless, highly reflective glass. In the center was a twenty-foot-diameter circular crystal, a foot high, on which were three glowing glass seats. The middle seat was two steps higher than the others. On both sides of the seat were four, six-inch-diameter crystals of different colors that rose from the floor up to the height of the armrest.

Supreme Commander Zork entered the room his two chancellors. They were from the dying planet, Trition, located in a galaxy just outside our Milky Way. Zork took the center seat with his chancellors taking their places on either side of him.

In physical form, they were nearly transparent, ghostly in appearance, glowing blue. Thread-like veins sparked white electricity through their bodies. Their physical form resembled that of humans: they had arms, legs, chests, and even possessed facial characteristics similar to those of humans. If it weren't for their transparent, ghost-like appearance and white veins, by human standards, they would be thought to be quite attractive in appearance.

Supreme Commander Zork motioned with his hand for Bellarouse to step forward.

"Earthling," he said.

Bellarouse shook her head, looking sorely

displeased for him missing her supreme name. "Master Cook, my name is Master Cook! Not "Earthling"… Supreme Dork!" she replied, placing emphasis on the word "dork."

"Zork, Supreme Zork!" said the commander. Elevated levels of electricity sparked through his body. He flashed his finger at Bellarouse and sent a jagged beam of electricity, resembling a miniature lightning bolt, at the base of her feet. She jumped. He smiled, then put his finger out and sparked another bolt of electricity at her. She jumped again, then started to dance.

"A million light year pardons for missing your prime ingredient right name, Supreme Zork," said Bellarouse, dancing her breath away.

"Hear now," said Zork, with a very serious look about him, as he continued to throw fits of lightning, "What are you doing?"

"I'm dancing the lightning bolt two-step, a recipe dance of mine. I just dreamed it up from the Milky Way for you, Supreme Zork."

"Well, now, I do like to be entertained," he said nodding, revealing a hint of a grin.

The sparking in his body started to go away once he'd heard Master Cook's apology and saw her entertaining dance steps.

"Never a dull taste bud with Master Cook at your service," she said, quickly running out of steam. "That's my motto." She suddenly found herself completely out of breath and had to stop dancing. "I can only last so long. A million light year pardons again, Supreme Zork." She bowed before him, then slowly looked up, all the while hoping he would stop sparking so much electricity. It was really starting to make her feel overly zingy.

Zork took a deep breath, leaned forward, and stared deeply into Bellarouse's eyes. "Well now, what is this Dork, as you mentioned?"

Bellarouse smiled. "Dork is a toasty buttered title of supreme earth intelligence," she said, pointing her fingertip at the side of her head. "They don't blend like cream and sugar. They stand out, special!"

Zork scratched his chin in a moment of silence. "Hum, interesting." His eyes narrowed. "Now then, Master Cook, what progress has been made in finding surrogate bodies for my people, and pets for entertainment?"

Bellarouse cleared her throat. "Everyday I have my pet caretaker find new sweet bodies and pets for your supreme recipe takeover," she said, rubbing her hands together.

He nodded and smiled, "Good, Master Cook. Now then, if this test proves successful and we find Earth to our liking," he waved his hand in a long sweeping motion before her, "I will signal for all our other fleets to land and occupy every major city on this planet." He clenched his hand in a tight fist.

"Then, we will take it over and claim it as our own."

Bellarouse took two steps forward, having a concerned look about her. "What about me, your Master Cook, and my sweet cake daughter? How do I know you won't take our bodies and soup out our intelligence into some pet for your entertainment too?"

Zork leaned forward in his chair. "Well now, we will still need some earthlings intact, in their own bodies to teach us so much more about your planet than what we have learned by studying you from space. Now then, prove yourself useful, and live."

"What happens if there aren't enough animals for you to put human intelligence into?"

"Well then, we possess a substance that can turn people into animals according to how they are in character—pigs, goats, dogs, even lions, but this is not the time for that."

Her eyes stretched wide. "If you don't act fast, this town is going hog wild."

"What does this mean, hog wild?" said Zork, leaning forward, squinting deeply into her eyes.

"In simple recipe talk, the whole planet will soon be stewing mad if you don't have the bodies you took over reappear back in town. Where's Albert and Sheriff Gary?"

Zork passed his palm over a blue crystal. In response, a ten foot-wide section of dome illuminated the bodies of Albert and Sheriff Gary lying motionless on crystal platforms in a state of suspended animation.

Zork continued, "Well now, my people have yet to decide which of them will adopt these bodies as their own."

Bellarouse took two steps forward. "The dough is rising fast." "You'd better act now, Supreme Zork."

Zork grinned. "Your primitive civilization has no hope in defeating us!"

Bellarouse bowed before Zork, then slowly raised her head. "No, Supreme Zork, but unless you want a world war—a scrambled egg planet, whipped into a useless mess of mass destruction, you must make sure your new human body counterparts blend in with all the others. Learning to copy their personalities is so very important if you want to keep your secret from being canned."

"Well then, can you help us... blend in, as you say?" he said, leaning forward in his seat, eyes narrowing.

"Help you?" said Bellarouse, grinning. "Why, with my Master Cook recipes, I'll make your stay here on planet earth a gravy train delight."

Zork narrowed his eyes. "Now then. How do we accomplish this?"

Bellarouse waved her hands about. "I know every two-bit, pea-body personality in this town, and how their supposed to act." She put her hand over her heart. "I was in cooking theatrics during my tender basting years. I will make and send out training videos on how each one of your new adopted bodies should behave in order to blend in."

Zork nodded. "Good. My subjects will be awaiting these videos of yours."

A sentry entered the room and whispered something into his ear.

"Well now, Master Cook," said Zork. "It appears that two young humans are outside this very moment spying your house."

"Oh…is that so!" Bellarouse rubbed her hands together. "Let's have a look-see!"

Zork passed his palm over a red crystal. A view of her back lot appeared through a section of the dome wall showing a young man and woman crouched behind her hedge.

"Well then." He closed his hand into a tight fist. "Snare those two, and put their bodies in with the others!"

Bellarouse flashed her hand up. "Wait, Supreme Zork," she said, recognizing one of them. "That young man is a relative fruit of mine. His name is Charlie. He's assisting me with the pet sitting operation. As for the girl, I don't know if she's a rotten apple or not." She turned toward Zork. "Don't take them yet," she said. "He's still very much a useful ingredient to my recipe, and for your supreme takeover plan. Since she is with him, let me investigate first to find out if they know anything before toasting her."

"Very well, Master Cook, let your Charlie continue to help find new bodies and pets, but just a short time longer."

"Supreme Zork… Charlie has a lunch appointment with me this next Saturday. I will make sure his friend comes along, then I will discover for myself if those two peas out there know anything about your sweet pod of a plan."

"Very well…agreed."

"Just one more thing, Supreme Zork," she said, "What if one of your soldiers mistakes me or my daughter for someone else? What will keep our minds from being sandwiched into some animal, and our beautiful bodies taken over as well?"

Zork motioned for one of his men to give her a case of crystal vials, each one filled with a glowing pink powder.

"Now then, swallow a pinch once a day. It will keep you both safe from harm."

Bellarouse bowed before him. "Thank you, Supreme Zork."

* * * * *

Bellarouse crept up behind Charlie and Holly as they spied her cornfield. "What are you doing here! Charlie!" she shouted.

Charlie and Holly looked back in shock, seeing Bellarouse standing right behind them. Charlie was so stunned by her sudden appearance he found himself unable to think of anything to say.

Bellarouse stretched her mouth open again, "And who's this?" she shouted, pointing at the girl crouched beside him.

Before Charlie or Holly had the chance to utter a word, Bellarouse sounded off again, "I'm asking you! Answer me!" Her eyes darted back and forth between the two of them. "What are you two doing here?"

Charlie finally found his voice. "Uh… Aunt Bellarouse. After telling my good friend here, Holly, about all your cooking trophies and blue ribbons, she said she just had to see them and you in person."

Bellarouse placed her hands firmly on her hips. "Oh…is that so?"

"I told her she might even be lucky enough to get your autograph. If that might be possible?"

"What? Oh my autograph is it!" Bellarouse looked pleasantly surprised. "You say she wants my autograph?" That moment her chest broadened, shoulders arched back, arms flexed big.

Holly heard her neck crack as she snapped her head to one side. *Does this lady lift weights or what?* she thought.

Bellarouse faced them dead on. "Now where abouts did this friend of yours come from?"

"She just moved to Kingston," said Charlie. "We attend the same high school, and are on the same debate team too."

"High school? Woo...and the debate team. How impressive! Well, I must insist then you bring your debating friend along for this Saturday brunch. Then...we'll talk autographs."

Charlie looked over at Holly. "Can you make it?"

"Why...pass up an invitation to visit the greatest culinary cook in the world! Of course I can make it! I wouldn't miss it for anything! As a matter of fact, I'll probably be dreaming about getting a taste of your aunt's blue-ribbon cooking every night."

Bellarouse grinned. "Well then. It's settled. And don't be late!"

CHAPTER 11

The following week, Holly and Charlie headed down the dirt road that led to Bellarouse's house for their Saturday afternoon luncheon. All of sudden, a black speck appeared down the road, just over the hill in front of them.

"I wonder what's that?" said Holly, squinting. "Can't make it out."

Charlie kept both eyes focused on the fast-approaching object until it became recognizable; a mixed-breed dog with matted fur. Charlie smiled at Holly. "That's Dumpster."

"Dumpster?" she said looking amused. "Who's Dumster?"

"The town's garbage moocher," he said, chuckling.

No sooner had he finished those words, Dumpster raced by, leaving a cloud of dust behind him.

Charlie fanned the dust away from his face. "I

never saw that dog move that fast before. Something must have really spooked him, or else he got wind of some super good food someone just took out to the garbage. People around town know that if they take some fresh leftover pizza out to the trash Dumpster will pick up the scent and be in front of their place in forty minutes or less, depending on where he is at the moment."

"Gee. Talk about quick garbage disposal. Dumpster sounds pretty efficient."

Twenty minutes later, Holly and Charlie arrived at Bellarouse's house just in time to keep their lunch appointment.

Charlie turned and faced Holly, "Remember, try to include as many food words as you can while talking with my aunt. Eating and cooking is her whole life. As you know, she has a food vocabulary all her own."

Holly smiled, "Oh, I get it. You want me to show off my fruitcake personality to get on her sweet side."

"Well….yes." he said. "I think that would help."

Right as Charlie was about to knock on the front door, it suddenly opened in front of him. Bellarouse smiled at them from behind the screen door. "Well, well, how scrumptious of you to show up. Welcome! Welcome! Come right inside."

The floorboards in Bellarouse's living room creaked beneath their feet as they followed her lead toward the dining area. Heading down the hallway, they observed a wide assortment of gold framed photographs showing off a variety of award-winning dishes. Bellarouse was in the center of all the pictures, holding a blue ribbon or trophy over her head. The frames were kept so clean that Holly had to squint as she walked past to keep from being blinded by the reflection of the ceiling lights off the glass covers.

When Holly entered the dining room, she couldn't hardly imagine the depths of Bellarouse's cooking world. From every direction were photographs of her holding trophies and first place blue ribbons. She gazed down at the placemats and tablecloth, taking note that everything was silk-screened with images of first-place awards. There were six, gold leafed ceramic mugs on the table that said, "I'm Number One" in large bold letters.

In the middle of the black mahogany dining table was a huge gold-plated chicken trophy. Bellarouse came up behind Holly and placed her hand firmly on her shoulder. "That, my dear woman, is my pride and joy. The Pulitzer Prize for the world's best chicken stew recipe. Isn't it just amazing?"

"Yes… very, very impressive," said Holly.

Holly stepped over to Charlie and whispered into his ear. "She sure has lots of first place cooking plaques. The only plaque I have is on my teeth."

Bellarouse gave Holly a quick sneer. "Oh, Holly,

it's not polite to whisper. Especially in front of your host!"

Holly nodded, looking a little embarrassed.

"Sit up straight, Charlie!" said Bellarouse, "You know I don't like slackers at the table!" Her face suddenly flashed between Holly and Charlie. "Do you two like taking night walks, out in the field?" she said in a whispery tone of voice.

"I'm not the night owl type, really," said Holly, "if that's what you're hinting at."

Bellarouse stepped over to the kitchen table and served them two plates of her favorite dish.

"Aunt Bellarouse," said Charlie, "you really out did yourself. This looks and smells delicious."

Right, looking good!" said Holly, giving her a thumbs up. "Shepherd's pie. I love shepherd pie!"

"Good. Good." Bellarouse brought over two large bowls of her famous clam chowder. After they finished all the food, Bellarouse leaned close to Holly and whispered into her ear, "Tell me truthfully now, are you a corn stalker?"

"Uh…stalker?" she said, "Uh, what's that suppose to…?"

"You know what I mean. Like going into people personal crops and stalk for things?"

"Things? Me? Absolutely not!"

Charlie cleared his throat to get his aunts attention. "This was the most awesome brunch ever, Auntie. I totally forgot. One of your clients asked me if I could do some pet sitting for them an hour earlier than normal."

"Well now Charlie. It's a shame to hear that you and your friend have to leave so early." Bellarouse walked up to Holly and pinched her cheek, "Be sure to join us again soon?"

Holly gave Bellarouse a big smile. "I would love to experience more of your awesome cooking!"

"Well good," she said, "Here's my autograph you asked for."

Holly gave an extra big smile for Bellarouse. "Wow! Thanks so much! I must have this framed so I can hang it in my room!"

Moments later, Charlie and Holly headed out the front door and back down the dirt road toward town

.

CHAPTER 12

At ten o'clock in the evening, Bellarouse peeped out of her room and looked down the dark hallway. She saw light beaming out from the beneath her daughter's bedroom door, and could hear her talking make believe with her dolls.

Bellarouse locked herself in her bedroom. "Now's a good time to do some serious video work for my alien friends." She mounted her video recorder to a tripod and beamed bright lights toward a director's chair placed on the far side of the room.

Next, she removed a black book from her desk drawer containing the names, addresses, and photographs of ten victims whose bodies had been taken over by the aliens. One by one, she went down the list, making videos of herself acting out the voice type, gestures, and attitudes of each person. She included information about where they worked, places where they liked to hang out, and their favorite clothes to wear.

After completing each video, she placed them into individual bags and wrote on the outside the address where they were supposed to be delivered.

"Just two more to go," said Bellarouse, feeling totally exhausted. She leaned forward in her director's chair, then took out her handkerchief and patted beads of perspiration off her forehead. The last two people on her list were Spike Bruster and Shirley Brentwood who lived on opposite sides of town.

Bellarouse smiled at the picture of Shirley. "Wow, what an angel cake," she said, beholding the thirty-two-year-old, part-time fashion model's flowing blond hair and shapely six-foot frame. Bellarouse started to videotape herself, giving instructions on how Shirley should act and talk.

"You are a fantastic giggler, and do it often. During the day, when you're out with people in general, you like to raise your forearm and flap your hand up and down, keeping your wrist steady. While giggling you say, 'Hee, hee hee. Oh my gosh, oh my gosh,' in a high-pitched voice right after you see anything that excites you. When you see a dog you say, 'What a cute puppy you are.' You are often seen in public shopping around town on rollerblades. You love Cha-Cha's Boutique and like to wear silk shirts and slacks patterned with lots of brightly colored tropical flowers and birds. Your all-time favorite place to eat brunch is at The Hot Pink Tortoise Restaurant, where you enjoy nibbling your food slowly, like a turtle. One of your trademarks is taking a flower from the table vase and placing it behind your left ear."

Next, Bellarouse opened her black book and stared for a moment at the photo of the last person on her list, Spike Bruster. She grimaced at the image of the coarsely shaven, burly, muscle-bound, forty-year-old suspected bank robber. She stood in front of the video camera and started to act out instructions on how he behaved, and what were his special interests.

"You're a tough dude. You walk straight and stiff, rocking your whole body from side to side, swinging your arms close to your hips, keeping them rigid as you move. You speak in a super low, raspy tone of voice. As you talk, your voice quickly gets louder. You're very fond of shopping at Roughriders Western Wear and like broad-rimmed cowboy hats, leather vests, pants, and pointy black leather boots. Your favorite place to hang out is Burt's Buffalo Restaurant. You usually order up prime rib, and when you eat you don't show very good table manners. Getting grease all over your face, and then wiping it off with the back of your arm is a special trademark of yours."

Early the next morning, Bellarouse stepped out onto her front porch holding her special bags, each containing the videos she had made the night before. After five minutes of waiting, she stared through the front screen door at the grandfather clock, and sighed.

She squinted down the road and said, "Where's that kid?" She finally saw her newspaper boy appear over the crest of the hill, pumping the pedals of his bike as he raced towards her house. Two half-filled newspaper sacks hung over his bike rack. A minute later, he suddenly squeezed his handle brakes and skidded to a stop by her front steps.

Bellarouse waved the dust away from her face. "Ricky! You're five minutes late!" she said, wagging her finger at him.

"Gosh, sorry," he said, glancing up into her grimacing stare.

"If you want to cut the mustard in this world, boy, you've got to be like clockwork. You get what I'm trying to say?"

"Yes, Ma'am."

Ricky noticed Bellarouse's large body rock side to side as she stepped toward him.

She leaned forward and glared down into his eyes. "I need these delivered to the addresses on the bags," she said, forcing a grin. "Think you can handle it?"

Ricky arched his shoulders back and took a

deep breath. "You can depend on me. Just curious… what's in the bags?"

"Secret recipes. That's all you need to know! Now here are the bags."

Ricky packed them tightly in his canvas sacks.

"Now it's very important," she said, pointing at his face, "that you make absolutely, positively make sure you deliver each bag to the correct right address. Got it?" She reached out and gripped his shoulder, staring down at him with a twisted grin.

Ricky jerked his shoulder free. "Piece of cake," he said, swiping the air. He mounted his bike and raised his chin. "Don't worry. I'm an expert delivery boy."

Bellarouse crossed two sets of fingers for good luck as she watched him race down the road until he disappeared over the crest of the hill.

A mile down the road, Ricky rode past a mixed-breed dog with matted fur who had its head stretched inside a rusted trashcan looking for food. The mutt heard something race by and popped his head out of the trash to check it out. He caught sight of Ricky on his bike and decided to take chase. Ricky looked back over his shoulder to see if the dog was still by the trash. To his surprise, he saw the mangy dog running right for him—fast. He recognized the dog as Dumpster, the town garbage moocher who got a bad reputation for scaring the neighbor kids by biting into their back tires, giving them flats, then chase them on foot. Ricky pumped his peddles hard and sped down the road as fast as he could. His cheeks jiggled as his bike bounced over a series of potholes in the road.

Ricky made a sharp turn down a grassy slope. When he reached the bottom of the hill, he made another sharp turn toward the sidewalk. His back tire slid out from underneath him, causing his bike to fall sideways onto the grass. He quickly got back up and looked back. Dumpster charged down the hill right at him. When the dog got within twenty feet, Ricky waved his arms high over his head to make himself look as big as possible and shouted in his loudest voice, "BACK OFF!"

The dog and boy stared at each other in a standoff of nerves for a few seconds. Ricky tried to bluff the dog by shouting some more, then charged right at him. To his surprise, Dumpster suddenly turned and ran back up the hill and disappeared from sight. Ricky gave a deep sigh of relief, but then grimaced, when he looked back and saw half of his newspapers and special delivery items scattered across the grass.

As he knelt down to repack he noticed that the contents of two of Bellarouse's special bags had completely slipped out. "Darn!" he said, not knowing for certain what item belonged to which bag with the correct address. After he finished repacking, he sped off on his bike to finish his deliveries.

CHAPTER 13

Later in the day, Ricky finished delivering the Aliens special instructional videos, including the two he thought he might have got mixed up. The aliens knew how important it was to pay attention to Bellarouse's instructions if their supreme leader's plan was to have any chance of succeeding.

The alien inhabiting Spike Bruster's body looked puzzled when he watched his video showing Bellarouse give instructions on how to be a fantastic giggler, flap his wrists, go shopping on rollerblades, and buy silk outfits patterned with lots of brightly colored flowers at a place called Cha Cha's Boutique.

Meanwhile, across town, the alien in Shirley Brentwood's body was equally puzzled when she viewed her video, giving instructions on how to be a tough dude and eat out at a place called Burt's Buffalo Restaurant and so on.

That morning, Supreme Commander Zork

received special high frequency transmissions from Spike and Shirley asking about their videos. They said there must have been some kind of mistake with regards to the instructions they were given on the videos. Zork, not having seen the videos personally, and having complete confidence in Bellarouse work, ordered them to follow her exact instructions.

Spike headed out the front door of his house toward town. After buying some cool looking rollerblades, he approached three men dressed in business suits, talking to each other on the street corner. Spike giggled as loud as he could. The three men slowly turned and stared at him stone-faced, not knowing what to think of the hairy dude on skates. Spike giggled and thanked them for telling him how to get to Cha Cha's Boutique.

At that same moment, on the other side of town, Shirley went out shopping and bought some western wear, including a broad-rimmed cowboy hat that had a silver dollar attached to the front. She rocked her body in rigid fashion, side-to-side, and walked with clenched fists, just as the video suggested. Feeling kind of hungry, she headed to Burt's Buffalo Restaurant wearing her new cowboy clothes.

On the front of Burt's restaurant was a fifteen-foot wide wood sign having twelve, three-foot high buffalos hand carved into the surface. They appeared to be stampeding straight ahead, feet flying forward. Two of the largest buffalos, one at each end, had eight-inch cast iron rings pierced through their nostrils. The building's walls were constructed of red brick, rough mortared, white cemented inside and out.

Charlie and Holly were out patrolling the streets, looking for any signs of Albert and other missing town folk. As they turned the corner, Charley was surprised to see Shirley step into Burt's restaurant dressed in cowboy clothes.

"How bizarre," said Charlie, "I know for a fact the lady that just stepped into that restaurant is a super model. She never dresses like that. Wild West food is not her cup of tea either."

"Burt's Buffalo Restaurant?"

"Yeah."

"Let's go see what she's up to."

The double front doors to Burt's Restaurant flapped back and forth behind Charlie and Holly as they stepped inside. After getting seated, Holly glanced over at Shirley, observing her standing just inside the front entrance, looking about, taking in the surroundings.

A waiter stepped up to their table. "Can I take your order?"

"We're still thinking," said Holly. "A couple glasses of water would do nicely for now."

Charlie gazed across the table at Holly. "How

about some heavenly buffalo wings?"

Holly leaned forward, eyes fixed on Charlie. "The town's turning upside down and you're talking wings?"

"Sorry."

Holly gazed up at the large menu hanging on the wall. It looked like old parchment—with kind of a burnt look around the edges. The menu read: Prime Buffalo Rib, Chuck Buffalo, Buffalo Wings and Buffalo Milk, which came with a written guarantee, by Burt the owner, to put hair on "anyone's" chest.

"Wow," said Holly, "this place even has buffalo milk guaranteed to put hair on my chest! I think I'll pass today. Freaky."

Shirley seated herself on a chair made from bent willow branches. The cushion was made from buffalo hide—with the hair and all. Next, she faced one of the waiters and blurted out in the loudest, deepest voice, "Hey, you got some good prime rib here?" After she gobbled down a plate of prime rib, she wiped the grease and sauce off her face with the back of her arm, just as the video she watched earlier suggested.

"I think we've seen enough here," said Holly. "Let's head out and do some more street patrol."

Charlie gave Holly a thumbs-up. After leaving Burt's, they headed south to check out the downtown shopping area.

That same moment, several blocks away, Spike

Bruster located the store he was looking for. Its neon lights flashed the words, Cha Cha's Boutique in bright green and pink colors. A sign hung by the front window that read, The "IN" Place for Trendy Wear. Spike parted strands of rainbow colored beads strung across the front door, then rollerbladed inside.

He raised his nose to the scent of tangy mango and guava scent, vaporized as a fine mist from two aromatherapy dispensers placed at each end of the shop. Cha-cha music filled the store as the customers did their shopping. Spike rollerbladed around several circular display racks until he spotted some nice looking silk outfits patterned with all sorts of exotic looking flowers and birds, just like the video suggested.

Cha Cha's Boutique had a pet Macaw parrot, named Sylvester, that liked to perch on the sales racks. The bird had a special talent for talking customers into buying Cha Cha clothes.

"You're special! Special price!" squawked Sylvester, in front of Spike, "You're special! Special price!" the parrot kept repeating.

Spike leaned back and giggled at Sylvester, then flapped his hand at the bird and said, "You're cute." Then he giggled some more.

After picking out a flashy flower design outfit he passed between two seven-foot-high artificial palm trees on his way to the dressing room. Inside he heard the sound effects of ocean waves while trying on his new clothes.

Moments later, Spike rollerbladed up to the cashier and smiled. He waved his hand at the wrist, then giggled while paying for his new silk outfit.

Charlie did a double take as he passed by the front window to Cha Cha's Boutique. He pulled Holly to the side and whispered into her ear, "I just saw Spike Bruster, a suspected bank robber and ex-con dressed in silk pants and top—on rollerblades!"

Holly caught a glimpse of Spike standing by the register. Charlie pulled her back. "Don't stare!"

"What? Just one more peak. He looks like kind of a tough dude beneath the silk."

"You remember the oldie song, "Macho Man"?"

Holly nodded.

"That's the guy."

"Maybe he turned retro macho."

Spike burst out between the beads at the front entrance and rollerbladed by.

"Let's tail that chick… I mean…guy," said Holly.

"Right," said Charlie, jogging by Holly's side as they tried to keep up with Spike on his rollerblades.

"Rollerblades are cool," said Holly, glancing over at Charlie.

"Yeah, but not on a hairy dude on wheels sporting Miss Silk Tropic fashions!"

They stopped to watch Spike rollerblade up to a woman who was walking her French poodle. He knelt in front of her dog and giggled. "Hee, hee, hee. Oh my gosh, oh my gosh," he said in a high-pitched voice. He stared up at the woman and said, "What a cute puppy you have!"

The lady shook her head and pulled her dog out of his reach.

Holly laughed, then looked over at Charlie, "Macho man you said?"

"This town is turning retro gender," said Charlie.

Minutes later, they watched Spike rollerblade up to The Hot Pink Tortoise Restaurant and step inside.

"That looks like a cool place to eat," said Holly, pointing at the sign by the front entrance, which read, "The Best Slow Dining Experience in the South!"

"Better take slow bites in there," said Charlie.

"Absolutely. Wouldn't want to ruin their reputation."

Their eyes stretched wide the instant they entered the restaurant. The interior was decorated with tropical plants and flowers. The menus, napkins, seat cushions, bread and salad bowls were all patterned with pink tortoise shell designs.

Just outside, town folk gathered in front of the restaurant and stared in through the window, gawking at Spike Bruster's new silk outfit.

Holly and Charlie seated themselves a couple

tables away from Spike. They watched him call over a waiter by flapping his wrist. Next, he removed a Hibiscus flower from the table vase and placed it behind his left ear. Spike knew he was being watched. He looked back over his shoulder at Holly and gave her a sweet sandpaper face smile.

Charlie put his hand to his forehead. "This can't be happening! It looks like Mr. Silk Fashion Man might have a silk tropic crush on you, Holly."

"Don't be jealous, Charlie boy," she said grinning, "He's not my type. I like real macho men like you." Holly leaned across the table and gave Charlie a kiss.

Charlie blushed. "Gosh Holly, thanks. I didn't know I was that much macho."

Holly and Charlie decided to leave The Hot Pink Tortoise and head out to look for more clues.

* * * * *

It only took about two hours for the Kingston gossip society to spread the news about Spike and Shirley's bizarre behavior all over town. Bellarouse felt faint the instant she got word of the news. "How could he! How could he mess things up… so… so badly!" she mumbled to herself. Her hand shook and eyes narrowed as she dialed the number to Ricky's house.

"Oh, hello, Bellarouse," said Ricky's mom. She

detected some tension in her voice. "Is Ricky in some kind of trouble?"

"Of course not," said Bellarouse. "I just wanted to thank him for the "great job" he did in delivering my paper."

"Ricky's home now. I'll put him on. I'm sure he'll love to hear your compliment."

"Oh, hello…Ricky," said Bellarouse.

Ricky sensed some irritation in her voice. "Gosh, I hope nothing's wrong."

"Wrong? Why should there be anything wrong?"

Ricky stuttered. "I… I had a stupid accident."

"Stupid accident?" said Bellarouse, with a sigh. She felt lightheaded and sat down.

"Yeah, like this dog chased me." Ricky chuckled, trying to make it sound not so serious. "I lost my balance and everything fell out. Yeah, and two of your bags might have got mixed up… just a little."

"Just a little?" she said.

Bellarouse became silent for several seconds.

"Hello? Mrs. Haggerty… are you still there?"

Bellarouse suddenly spoke up, "Just a little?" she repeated.

Ricky took a deep swallow. "I was chased by this dog." His voice suddenly sounded really nervous. "He's the one to blame for everything."

"Dog? What dog is this?" she said, fisting her hand tight.

"The mutt who mooches the town trash," he said, with a chuckle. "You know, Dumpster."

Bellarouse smiled. "Yes, yes, I know Dumpster dog. Come on over to my house in about three hours from now and I'll have a special bonus waiting for you. You should get everything you deserve. Oh… and don't fret yourself about that little accident either."

Ricky's eyebrows arched. "Bonus! Really? I'll be right over in three hours!"

Later that day Ricky ran out of his house and sped on his bike down the road toward Bellarouse's residence. About half way to her house, he rode past Charlie and Holly as they walked down the road.

"That's strange," said Charlie.

"What?" said Holly.

"I wonder why Ricky is in such a hurry, especially when he's heading toward Bellarouse's house."

"Well the Druskys live that way too."

"Yes, but he doesn't deliver papers there. He might be heading to Bellarouse's house. Maybe to collect some money. He could be in danger. We'd better check on him."

"Right!" she said.

Minutes later, Ricky reached Bellarouse's house. She was already waiting for him on the front porch.

"Hi Bellarouse," said Ricky with a smile, getting off his bike by the front steps. "I've come to collect my reward." He stretched his hand out, expecting a nice tip.

"No, no! It's not here! Your reward is in my cornfield," she said, casting a lopsided smile, pointing back toward her field.

Ricky looked confused. His outstretched hand melted. "Cornfield? But what could be out there?"

"You'll love the great surprise I have there for you—a big bonus—just inside," she said, grinning, "Now go. Go on. Check it out! You'll love it."

"Well…" said Ricky, sounding not too convinced that a real prize could be waiting for him in her cornfield.

"Trust me," she said, pointing to her field.

A sudden smile sprouted on his face. "Well, okay," he said, with a big nod, rubbing his hands together.

Bellarouse gazed out her back window and watched Ricky run toward the cornfield. He stopped briefly and looked back at the house. Bellarouse waved out the window for him to continue. Ricky parted the six-foot-high stalks of corn to try and see his special surprise.

Charlie and Holly reached Bellarouse's house just in time to see Ricky enter the cornfield. They wanted to yell out for him to stop, but couldn't chance alerting Bellarouse.

"I've got to go in after him!" said Holly.

Charlie reached out and held her back. "You

might disappear too. I need you with me to help solve this mystery."

"I guess you're right."

Minutes later, they were startled to see Dumpster dog suddenly race out of the field with Ricky nowhere in sight.

"This scene looks way too familiar," said Holly.

"Poor Ricky," said Charlie, swaying his head side-to-side.

They peered through the bushes and watched Dumpster race toward the front of the house. Next, the dog did the most unusual thing. It jumped onto Ricky's bike and tried to put its front paws on the handlebars and hind legs on the pedals. He tried to get the bike moving, but his legs were too short and the bike ended up falling flat on its side. The dog raised his head toward the sky and howled.

Bellarouse stomped up to the edge of the steps and placed both hands firmly on her hips, squinting down at the dog. "I told you to be careful in delivering my goods!" she scowled. "This is your just reward for messin' up my work. My great plan!"

Tears started to swell up in the corners of the dog's eyes.

"You're nothing," she said, wagging her finger at him again. "How dare you mess up my plan! You'll never amount to anything!"

He slowly turned his mangy, hairy face toward Bellarouse and showed his yellow teeth while staring at her pudgy legs.

"Don't be showing those yellow choppers to me, Dumpster! You trash mutt. You're nothing more than a dumpster dog now, Ricky boy!"

Dumpster stepped her direction with his head hung low. Tears dripped down his matted face, stained with pizza sauce from digging in someone's trash earlier that day. He raised his muzzle and displayed his yellow teeth at Bellarouse.

She leaned forward, hands on her knees, and glared down at him. "You're nothing! You'll never amount to anything! Ever! Ever!"

He slowly raised his head and took another step toward her legs, then another, and another. Bellarouse stepped back, then suddenly turned and made a mad dash inside her house, slamming the door shut behind her. Just outside, she could hear Dumpster in a wild rage, pawing and ripping her screen door to pieces.

Out behind the bushes, Holly put her hand to her mouth. "Looks like Dumpster's revenge!"

Charlie sighed. "Or Ricky's."

CHAPTER 14

Bellarouse had an unusual feeling that she was being watched when she reached into the oven to remove one of her pies. She was right. Seconds earlier, one of Zork's special messengers had silently passed through the wall to her kitchen and was now standing directly behind her.

"Bellarouse!" shouted the messenger.

She was so startled by his voice her arms flew up, and so did the pie. It almost hit the ceiling before it descended and splattered across the kitchen floor in front of her feet.

Bellarouse leaned back against the stove in shock as she faced the alien. "Get out of my house!" she shouted, taking a giant step forward. "You can't touch me… or my daughter," she continued, pointing at herself. "I'm under the protection of your commander, Supreme Zork!"

The alien grinned. "His Excellency requests your presence… immediately."

Bellarouse reluctantly slipped on her black leather boots and headed out the back door with the alien following close behind.

Moments later, she entered the domed room where Zork was waiting for her in his crystal chair. He stared at her with narrowed eyes.

"Supreme Dork!" Bellarouse blared.

"Zork!" he said, looking sorely displeased. "Supreme Zork!"

Bellarouse bowed before him. "A million light year pardons, Supreme Zork."

Her mouth suddenly dropped open in shock, seeing Spike Bruster and Shirley Brentwood standing at the far side of the room. Spike was wearing his flowery women's clothes, while Shirley had on her cowboy attire. Her hair, face, and right arm was covered with prime rib sauce. Bellarouse's face drained of color as she slowly looked back into Zork's piercing eyes.

"Well now, Master Cook," said Zork, leaning forward. Bellarouse noticed twice the amount of electricity sparking through his veins.

"How then, do you explain this?" said Zork, pointing at Shirley and Spike.

Bellarouse looked back and forth between Spike, Shirley, and Zork in silence.

Zork squinted at Bellarouse. "Now then, is this

what you call blending in?" He waved his palm over a blue crystal. One of his subjects entered the room holding two cats in his arms.

Bellarouse pointed at the furry creatures. "What are those two cream puffs for?"

Zork leaned forward, with a stone-face expression. "Your usefulness here has expired!"

"You… you… you… you're not putting the queen of cooks into one of those hair balls!" she said, taking a small step forward.

"You see," said Zork, getting up from his chair, "not only you, but your daughter too!"

Bellarouse squeezed her eyes shut and sighed. A second later, her eyes stretched wide open. "Wait, Supreme Zork! I just thought of a marvelous plan to get everyone… the whole town…gathered in one place…with enough animals to transfer their minds into all at the same time!"

"Now then, how is this possible?"

"Tomorrow is the grand opening for the town's new zoo. It will be an early evening zinger of an occasion, with free admission and food. The whole apple dumpling town, together with exotic animals from all over this pear shaped planet will be there, all in one place."

Zork thought in silence for a moment. "Well, perhaps I was too hasty, Master Cook. Now then, I will give you one more chance. But don't fail me again!"

Bellarouse raised her finger. "Wait… One last thing, Supreme Zork."

"Well then, yes?"

"I don't want anything to go sour wrong again. Be sure to keep an eye on Charlie, and especially his friend, Holly, at the zoo. I suspect they might know more than what they let on. We don't want any surprise event to spoil your supreme takeover plan."

Supreme Zork passed his hand over his yellow crystal. "I have just the subject to accomplish your request, Master Cook." At that moment, Sheriff Gary's alien takeover body stepped into the room.

"This is Eros," said Zork. "He will see to it."

Bellarouse looked over at Eros with a smug grin, then gave Zork a nod of approval

CHAPTER 15

Awhispering voice called out Holly's name as she lay in bed.

"Miss Holly," said Stephanie. "I have important news."

Holly's eyes sprung open. "Stephanie! she said, in an excited tone of voice. "What is it? What did you discover?" Before she had the chance to answer, her twin sister, Agatha, started to pass through the door. She smiled warmly at them, continuing forward, but before making it all the way through, suddenly jolted back. Her left arm looked as if it was stuck on the other side of the door. She yanked and pulled it, but it wouldn't budge. Holly heard something rap against the opposite side of the door each time she pulled her arm forward.

Holly leaned forward. "Agatha, are you all right? What's wrong with your arm? And what's that noise?"

She giggled and blushed. "Oh, I almost forgot for a moment... a moment," then giggled again. "I'll be right back." She disappeared and quickly reentered, this time by opening and closing the door. She was carrying a glass vial filled with a glowing pink powder.

Holly quickly got out of bed. "What's that you're holding?"

"Miss Holly," said Stephanie, with a warm smile, "it will keep you safe."

"Safe... yes safe," said Agatha, shadowing her sister's speech.

"Safe? Safe from what?" Holly, glanced back and forth between the two of them. "From whom?"

"From them—from them, the ones you spoke of," said Agatha.

"The alien ghosts?"

They nodded.

"Wow! Something from another galaxy. I could never have imagined in my wildest dreams that I'd actually be holding something like this."

"Forgive us, Miss Holly," said Stephanie, "but at first we thought you were, you see, a little..."

Agatha giggled and looked Holly straight in the eye. "Crazy, Holly... crazy."

Holly grinned. "Crazy?"

"Miss Holly, the idea of ghosts from other planets," said Stephanie.

Agatha's expression suddenly became very serious. She stared into Holly's eyes. "Kingston and the whole planet is in grave danger... danger, you see."

"We saw them in Bellarouse's house," said Stephanie, casting a worried look.

"Alien ghosts?" said Holly, stepping closer.

They both nodded.

"They didn't see you... did they?"

"No, we waited till they left... then took some."

"The powder?"

They nodded.

"Miss Holly, take a pinch a day. It will keep you safe. They won't be able to take your body, you see," said Stephanie. "They're putting the minds of people they take over into animals."

"Of course!" said Holly, snapping her fingers. "I suspected it for some time. That explains a lot."

Stephanie appeared confused. "Miss Holly. What do you mean?"

"The Drusky's pig, Button Rouge, I believe is their son, Albert."

"Albert?" said Agatha.

"I believe his body has been taken over and his mind is now in the pig, Button Rouge. That also explains why several other people in town are acting weird and their pets are behaving super smart."

"Tomorrow, Miss Holly," said Stephanie, "they're planning on taking over the bodies of everyone in town!"

Holly's eyes bulged wide. "But how... where? Don't they need lots of animals to put the human minds into?"

"Correct, Miss Holly. They will strike right after dusk," said Stephanie.

Agatha stepped in front of Holly. "At the new zoo... the zoo!"

"But how are we going to stop them?" said Holly.

The twins glanced at each other with blank stares, then looked back at Holly.

"Please, I need more help, more information. Can you do more spying for me?"

They nodded.

"They must have a weakness," said Holly. "There must be a way to destroy them, or at the least make them want to leave our planet for good."

"We will try to help," said Stephanie, nodding.

"Yes help... help," echoed Agatha.

"Can you think of anything else? Any bit of information that might be of use?"

Stephanie looked blankly at the wall for a moment, then looked back. "Miss Holly, they did mention that Kingston is an experiment. If it goes well, you see, if they like it here, then the rest of the planet will be next."

"Yes, Holly," said Agatha. "You see… you see."

"Can you get more of this protective powder?" she said, peering at the vials glowing contents.

They shook their heads.

"This is only enough for me, and perhaps one other person, for a few days."

"Miss Holly, we dare not try to get more."

"Yes, yes," said Agatha. "We dare not get more, more."

"We will return. We hope with more information, soon," said Stephanie. "Till then, good-bye Miss Holly, and good luck."

"Yes, good-bye… bye," said Agatha, waving.

Holly watched the twins float across the floor, then disappear from sight through her bedroom wall.

Holly got on the phone to call Charlie and told him all about her encounter with the twin ghosts and what she had learned about the aliens. She explained that she only had enough of the protective powder for the both of them, and perhaps their families for a day or two. She told him that she was now convinced that Button Rouge "the pig" has Albert mind and his body is somewhere else. She said the aliens were planning a big attack right after dusk at the new zoo, and it was very important to do everything possible to convince family members and anyone else they could not to go.

They agreed to share the protective powder,

then meet again the following day for the zoo's grand opening ceremony, hoping to have some plan in place by then to get the people out of harm's way before the attack at dusk.

CHAPTER 16

The following day Charlie and Holly met at the Kingston Zoo for the grand opening ceremony. They stood toward the back of a large crowd of town folk, facing the zoo's front entrance where Mayor Paul Jenkins was busy broadcasting his dedication speech over the loud speakers.

"I don't know how we're going to stop it," said Charlie. "Perhaps once we get inside…"

"If things don't go well…" said Holly. She pointed back over her shoulder toward the exit.

"Just curious. What's in the large handbag you're carrying? Looks pretty heavy."

"Newspaper… and lots of it."

"Newspaper?"

"In case things don't go well later on, I have kind of a crazy idea how we can use it to our advantage."

"Care to share?"

"Can't talk about it now with all the people around. I'll tell you more after we get inside."

"I couldn't keep my parents from coming," said Charlie, looking about to see if he could spot them in the crowd. "I know they're here somewhere. I couldn't tell them the truth. Who would believe me?"

Holly sighed. "I couldn't keep my parents from coming either. I didn't think your parents were the zoo type."

"They're not. It's just that several of my dad's clients are here, and he felt obligated to join in and try to have a good time."

Holly glanced into Charlie's eyes. "You took that special powder I gave you, didn't you?"

"Yep, I'd do anything to avoid having my mind put into a creepy zoo animal."

"Were you able to get your family to take a spiked drink of the powder?"

"Nope, except for Kent. At least he said he did."

"You didn't see him actually drink it?"

He hesitated a moment. "I told him that if he didn't drink it, I would tell his dad about his night prowl."

"Night prowl?"

"My crazy brother snuck out in the middle of

the night and hopped the fence to the zoo."

"But why?"

"He said to map out the place in his mind so on opening day he could impress his Montana girlfriend, Patricia."

"Impress?"

"You know, be like, Mr. Super Guide—show her what's cool, and what's not. How about your parents? Did you get them to take some?"

Holly shook her head. "By the time I was through trying to reason with them not to go, they'd already finished lunch and weren't agreeable to try anything weird looking, especially coming from me. I'm hoping somehow the twins will come through with new information that will help us in time. Pinch me, Charlie."

"What?"

"Go ahead. Pinch me!"

Charlie reached out.

"Not back there, silly."

She felt a slight pinch on her left arm.

"I was afraid of that."

"What?"

"This isn't a dream."

Just then, by the zoo entrance, the mayor was finishing his ceremony speech.

"Now, it is with great pride," said the mayor through the loudspeaker, "that I wish to present to you… the brand new Kingston Zoo! And, just as advertised… there'll be free admission and BBQ dinners for everyone! Have a wonderful time!"

Minutes later, the zoo grounds were filled with popcorn-munching, hamburger-toting visitors.

Thirty Minutes Till Dusk

Kent found his girlfriend standing by the refreshment stand. "Hey Patricia," he said, stepping up to her. "Hang out with me. I know all the best places to see."

"Well," said Patricia. "The best sights? OK, let's go."

Kent took Patricia's hand and guided her over to see the baby hippo exhibit first. They stood next to a mom holding her four-year-old daughter in her arms.

"Look! Look, Beth!" said the mom, smiling at her daughter. She pointed toward a mother hippo with her baby. "See the cute baby?"

Beth looked back and forth between her bottle and the hippo. Then, without warning, she flung her bottle over the fence. "Got Milk?" she shouted, watching it fly into the pool. The splash caught the baby hippo's attention. It swam right over to the bottle, stretched its mouth wide open and swallowed it whole. A mixed state of amusement, fear and panic followed.

"Call the zookeeper!" yelled one mother.

"Get the veterinarian!" shouted a man.

A large crowd swarmed around the exhibit and watched the zoo workers operate a large crane to hoist the baby hippo out of the pool and into the back of a large truck. The head veterinarian—Patricia's uncle, Dr. Spencer, quickly appeared on the scene and gave the hippo a quick examination, making sure its airways were clear before transporting it to the zoo hospital for continued observation and x-rays.

Kent looked over at Patricia. "Hey, I bet your uncle would let us inside the hospital. I know exactly where it is! Really!"

"Well, uh, yeah, I don't know." said Patricia with a smile. "We could try. Okay!"

"Let's go for it, really. Just follow my lead," said Kent. He took her by the hand and pulled her through the crowd toward the hospital.

At that same moment, at the west end of the zoo, Frank Drusky kept a close watch on his teary eyed wife, Annabel.

"I don't know if it was a good idea taking you here," said Frank. He put his arms around her shoulder.

"I'm glad you brought us," said Annabel.

Her son, Lance, watched the elephants toss dirt onto their backs for a moment, then glanced back over his shoulder at his mom. "Can we stay longer?"

Annabel cast him a warm smile. "Of course.

There's lots more animals to be seeing this evening."

"Stay longer?… Longer!" said his sister, Meagan. "Filthy, dirty animals. Smells worse than our pigs here." She tugged on her mom's sweater, "We just have to leave, now!"

Frank led his family to a secluded grassy spot on the side of a hill overlooking the gorilla and hyena exhibits.

"Here, this seems to be a good place to picnic," said Frank, smiling.

* * * * *

Holly and Charlie stood atop the zoo's highest hill. From their vantage point, they could almost see everyone in town having a great time eating and strolling from exhibit to exhibit.

Charlie shook his head in disappointment. "I guess the twin's weren't able to get any new information to help us out."

"I think you're right Charlie. I can think of only one thing that might get the people out in time before nightfall. A state of panic, instead of picnic."

"Panic? What sort of panic did you have in mind?"

"I need you to help me get those three trashcans moved close together and filled up with my newspaper."

"You're not thinking about…?"

"Yep. You better believe it. If we could get a big enough fire in those cans, it just might start enough of a panic to get everyone out of the zoo in time before the attack."

"It's a crazy idea," said Charlie, "but I guess we don't have any other choice."

After the trashcans were filled with wadded newspaper, Holly stepped up to the first container and lit a match.

"Well," said Charlie, "I guess no news is good news. I hope."

Just as she was about to set the newspaper on fire, someone reached out from behind and grabbed her arm. It was alien Sheriff Gary! He stared down at them with a smug grin.

"Didn't your mama teach you it's not safe to play with matches?" said Gary, reaching for his cuffs. "Did you really think you could stop us?"

Holly yanked her arm free, then lifted her leg and smashed the heel of her shoe onto the sheriff's foot as hard as she could. The sheriff bellied over in pain.

Charlie and Holly made a run for it, and sprinted down the hill. Within seconds, Sheriff Gary was in hot pursuit, running the best he could with a limp. He chased them all the way out to the zoo's main parking lot area, before being forced to stop to catch his breath.

Charlie noticed that his parent's car wasn't

parked where he saw it earlier, which made him think that they might have gotten it out in time.

They rested a moment in a thick grove of trees a couple hundred feet outside the parking lot.

Charlie leaned forward, out of breath. His arms rested on his knees. "What are we going to do now? They know. They're on to us!"

Holly clenched her fist. "We've got to get back inside… somehow. Let's try circling around."

They crouched low, and snuck around trees and behind bushes until they reached the rear service road. A ten-foot high chain-link fence blocked their way inside.

Holly walked up to the fence and looked back. "How are you at climbing?"

Charlie walked up beside her. "Let's do it."

They only got about six feet up the fence before they were spotted by three security guards. Holly noticed one of them grab his holster. The guards ran down the hill and shouted at them to freeze.

Holly and Charlie looked at each other for a second, then thrust themselves away from the fence. After tumbling down an embankment, they quickly rose to their feet and sprinted down the road to safety.

They decided it would be too dangerous to try and enter the zoo again. Instead, they agreed to make their way back to their respective homes to check on their families and meet up again later.

A Minute Before Dusk

Meanwhile, inside the zoo's emergency room, Kent and Patricia watched Dr. Spencer look over the baby hippo's throat and stomach x-rays.

"Well," said Dr. Spencer, with a sigh of relief. "There appears to be no blockage, and, as for the bottle, it should pass right through with the other roughage."

"Uh, yuck," said Patricia.

"Really, that's good news!" said Kent. He reached out and clasped Patricia's hand. Next, he gave her a big smile and led her over to the far side of the room so they could watch the baby hippo recover in its holding pen.

Dr. Spencer received a phone call from security. An officer stationed by the park's entrance warned him that the zoo was under attack by some unknown force. Dr. Spencer quickly stepped over to Kent and Patricia. "Listen carefully. There's some kind of trouble outside. Stay here. Don't leave till I get back! Understand?"

They nodded, then looked at each other with blank stares.

The moment Dr. Spencer left the room, Kent ran over to the door and peered out through the security window. His eyes stretched wide seeing beams of red light crisscross the night sky.

Just outside, the aliens were firing their mind-absorbing weapons at every human crossing their path. After taking over their bodies, they beamed the peoples' minds back into the different animals around the zoo.

CHAPTER 17

Back inside the Kingston Zoo Hospital, Patricia and Kent heard screams coming from just outside.

Patricia gripped Kent's shoulder. "What's happening?" she said in a panicked voice.

Kent kept staring out the window with bulging eyes.

"Kent, what's wrong! Answer me! What do you see!"

Before Kent had the chance to say a word, two aliens passed through the wall and fired their weapons at them, sending their bodies slumping to the floor. The aliens disappeared like vapors and passed into Kent and Patricia, taking over their bodies.

The alien who took over Patricia aimed his

weapon at the baby hippo, transferring her mind into it. The other alien looked about for a moment, then suddenly spotted a mouse dart out from a hole and run along the edge of the wall. He flashed his weapon at the tiny creature, sending Kent's mind into it. Patricia and Kent's bodies, inhabited by aliens, then left the hospital.

Patricia shook her hippo head. "What happened? I feel so bloated. Freaky! What am I doing in this pen?" She looked cross-eyed at her nose. "Uh, oh my gosh, oh my gosh! This can't be happening! Uh, yeah… this must be a dream!" she said, trying to calm herself. She started to panic and rushed forward and backward, bumping her mouth and behind against the pen railing trying to get out. "Ouch!" she said, feeling her bruises. "This isn't a dream! This isn't a dream! Help! Someone help me!"

Kent slowly moved his little mouse head about, trying to figure out why everything around him looked different. He was so small and everything around him suddenly appeared so big. Just as Patricia had done, he looked inward at his nose. The frightening sight caused the fur on the top of his head to stand straight up.

Patricia turned her head and caught sight of a mouse darting around the room, squeaking loudly, and running in circles.

"Kent. Where are you? Are you here?" shouted Patricia.

The mouse darted over to the hippo and looked up. "Patricia?"

The hippo looked down at the mouse. "Kent?"

"You got ripped," said Kent.

"Uh, me, yeah, but you got squeaky small."

"Those aliens!" he said, looking around the room. "Our real bodies! They're gone!"

"Uh, yeah, what are we going to do about it? I can't stay like this!" She stomped her right hippo foot on the concrete floor. "I want my real self back, and I want it back now!"

"First we need to figure a way out of here, and then maybe we can get some help."

She watched Kent scurry up the side of the concrete wall. "What are you doing?"

"We've got to work as a team." When he reached the height of her shoulders, he sprung away from the wall and landed on her back.

Patricia wiggled and twitched her body. "Oooh, that tickles. What are you doing?" she said, feeling Kent scurry across her back, then leap behind her left ear.

"I can be your guide and coach, really!" said Kent.

"Uh… I don't know."

"We can get through this."

"Uh yeah, is that possible?

CHAPTER 18

Kent the mouse jumped up and down for joy on top of Patricia the hippo's head after coaching her how to get out of the hospital by ramming the door down with her powerful body.

Patricia thundered down the lighted zoo pathway with Kent riding on her head. She heard monkey calls for help and stopped alongside the ape exhibit.

"The keys…" said a nearby chimpanzee. He stretched his arms out between the bars and waved them about. "Get the keys!"

An orangutan gripped his cage with his massive hands and tried to use his brute strength to bend the bars apart. "Set us free! Set us free!"

Kent scurried over to Patricia's ear and spoke

inside, "I know where the keys are. Just follow my directions."

"Right! Let's go."

About twenty minutes later, nearly all the animals in the zoo had been set free. Monkeys ran from exhibit to exhibit opening the last of the cages with the master keys.

As soon as they were all set free, the zoo animals met in the picnic area and formed a large circle. All the animals were present—elephants, lions, snakes, rhinos, hippos, bears, bobcats, giraffes, chimpanzees, gorillas, and orangutans, just to name a few.

Dr. Spencer had been turned into an African elephant; Mayor Paul Jenkins was a giant gorilla. The animals quickly recognized each other's voices even though, as animals, they spoke in their own natural voices: the laugh of a hyena, the growl of a lion, the snort of a hog. Happily, each animal was able to understand all the other species.

There was an uproar of arguing about what they should do next. Dr. Spencer raised his trunk and blew it loudly. It became so quiet you could hear a mouse squeak.

Mayor Jenkins, the gorilla, started to take control of the crowd. "We must divide up into groups," he said, beating his hairy chest, "That will make it more difficult for them to catch us."

A wild hog raised his snout and spoke up.

"Other cities must be warned about the aliens too," he squealed.

The mayor raised his hairy hands above his head. "We will all search for a way to get back our real bodies!"

"Here! Here!" said the rhino, raising her horn.

After much growling, beating of hairy chests, and pushing, the animals finally agreed to the mayor's plan to divide into small groups and head out in different directions.

* * * * *

Meanwhile, across town, Charlie sprinted up the front steps to his house, then flung the front door open. "Mom, Dad, Kent!" he shouted, but no one answered. He spotted a letter on the floor with his name written on it. He recognized his mom's handwriting. A sudden smile surfaced on his face as he started to read it. The message said his parents had a wonderful time at the zoo, and that they would be spending the evening at Uncle Jake's house. Charlie stared across the room in silence. They must have gotten out of the zoo before dusk for this letter to be here, he thought. "I just have to call to make sure."

Charlie picked up the phone and called his uncle. A moment later, he heard him pick up, "Hi, Uncle Jake," said Charlie. "could I please speak to my mom?" Charlie felt greatly relieved the instant he heard her voice. "How did you enjoy the new zoo?" he said.

"We had a great time, thank you."

"How long did you stay?"

"We decided to leave a little early so we'd have time to visit Uncle Jake this evening before heading back home."

Charlie took a deep breath. "Did you leave the zoo before dusk?"

"Why, yes…"

He sighed with relief. "That's cool."

"Why do you ask?"

"Oh, just curious."

After finishing his phone conversation, Charlie felt fairly certain that everything was okay with his family, and they made it out before the alien attack.

* * * * *

When Holly reached the front grounds to the McGuire mansion, she didn't see her parent's car parked in the driveway or garage. Her heart started pounding, thinking the worse. She ran into the house. "Mom… Dad!" she shouted. An eerie silence enveloped the mansion. She rushed from room to room, calling out for them, but they were nowhere in sight. Not even a whisper of hope could be heard anywhere. A feeling of dread overtook her.

She entered the basement and headed up the secret passageway. Upon entering the twins' attic she saw Stephanie and Agatha staring out the window toward the Mississippi. The lamp suddenly started to flicker light, growing stronger and brighter, until moments later, the entire room basked in its warmth.

"Stephanie! Agatha!" Holly called out.

The twins turned and faced her with worried expressions.

"Miss Holly," said Stephanie. "We knew you'd come!"

"Yes, come… come," said Agatha, with outstretched arms.

Holly walked up to them. "My mom and dad! Have you seen them?" Her voice was shaking. "Did you see them get out?"

They slowly shook their heads. "We're sorry, Miss Holly, everyone was trapped. No one escaped except the Drusky family. They got them too, later at their farm. They put their minds in their pigs."

"They were followed… followed," said Agatha, shaking her head. "Terrible… terrible!"

Holly's head sank low, then slowly looked up. "Do you know what happened to my parents? What kind of animals were they put into?"

They shook their heads.

"Sorry Miss Holly," said Stephanie. "We did see a group of animals heading toward a steamboat docked in the nearby town of Burton. You might try looking there first."

Holly took a deep sigh. "Thanks, I'll have Charlie help me look there. Did you learn anything else new? There must be a way to get their bodies back. The aliens must have a weakness. Can you help me?"

They both nodded.

"Miss Holly, we'll be back as soon as we get more news."

"Yes, news… news," said Agatha.

The twins waved good-bye, then turned and disappeared through the bedroom wall. At that same moment, the lantern's light faded to a tiny flicker.

CHAPTER 19

The streets in and around Kingston were so quiet you could hear a cricket chirp a block away. Down at city hall, however, the atmosphere was quite different. Light beamed out through the buildings many windows, acting like a giant lighthouse, attracting alien beings dressed in human bodies from miles around. It wasn't long before the entire parking lot was overrun with cars.

Aliens stepped out of their vehicles sporting their new planet-earth fashion bodies just as one would show off a new set of clothes. They grinned and smirked at each other with raised chins and eyes that glowed blue against the night sky. The walkway leading to the front doors were lined on both sides with magnolia trees speckled with giant blossoms. The aliens turned and looked up at the trees as they walked past, senses drawn to the flowers sweet fragrance.

Bellarouse entered the meeting hall and sashayed up the center aisle, casting smiley glances, acting as if she were the Queen of Sheba herself. She stepped behind the front podium, cleared her throat and looked into the crowd.

Everyone's attention was fixed on Bellarouse's every move. Beads of sweat formed on her forehead. She reached out for a glass of water and gulped it down. All ears listened attentively as she began to speak. She advised everyone on how to blend in, and how important it was for everyone to quickly memorize dates, names, places, and any other information they could find inside the humans' homes so they could be as close to the real person as possible. She said she knew practically every one of the faces in the crowd, and would personally help train and make them feel right at home here on planet earth.

Just then, someone burst in through the front doors. It was Deputy Smith. Everyone looked back and watched him run down the center aisle. The instant he reached the front podium he quickly turned around. His eyes bulged as he shouted, "The animals escaped! All the zoo animals escaped!" he repeated, "They fled into the countryside! I need everyone's help to try and capture them!"

Bellarouse waved her arms over her head to get

everyone's attention. "Listen," she bellowed. "The animals might try to warn other towns about you and spoil your supreme rulers' plan! They must be captured! Don't kill them. Lock them back in their cages. We don't want visitors from other towns to get suspicious seeing an empty zoo!"

All the people quickly got up from their seats and rushed toward the door, pressing shoulder-to-shoulder, hurrying as fast as they could to get back out into the parking lot. The streets suddenly came back to life as the aliens fired up their cars and headed out in search for the escaped animals. Several aliens drove back to the zoo to get trucks, cages, ropes, and nets to aid in the capture.

* * * * *

The westbound animals included: Dr. Spencer as a thirty-year-old African elephant, a younger male elephant, Mayor Jenkins as the Congo gorilla, Kent the mouse, Patricia the hippo, and other town folk turned animal—one large red-haired orangutan, a female rhino, and three chimpanzees who, before they were turned into chimps, had been known around town as the Boe brothers—Jim Boe, Ted Boe, and Fred Boe. They had a family business as clown entertainers. All the parents in town loved to hire them for kid's birthday parties. They were also stand up comedians and quite popular at various comic clubs throughout the other communities.

* * * * *

That evening, a riverboat dubbed "The Pinkerton" was docked by the town of Burton, located just a couple miles south of Kingston. Four minstrels—two men and two women dressed in black pants and long sleeved pleated white shirts played on the back deck. They picked their banjos, making some lively Mississippi bluegrass music. The Pinkerton's captain, Stuart Bremmer, stood on the second-level deck dressed in full uniform. He grinned down at his guests, and tapped his foot to the beat of the band's music.

A young bride wore a flowing white gown. Her groom sported a black tux, accented with a red bow tie. They formed the nucleus of a group of over seventy guests who gathered on the boat for their wedding reception. Seven people were seated to a table. They were served breaded catfish in Cajun sauce, cooked vegetables, and apple pie.

The bride gazed up into the night sky and dreamed of the stars as being countless clusters of sparkling diamonds. The sounds of laughter and loud conversation filled the air.

Unknown to the captain and guests of the Pinkerton, the westbound escaped animals had just spotted the lights of their steamer out in the distance from a nearby hill.

The adult African elephant—Dr. Spencer—swayed his trunk toward the younger elephant. "You stay here as lookout while we see if we can get some help from down there. Blow your trunk if you see the alien town folk coming, then stampede back to us."

The young elephant raised and lowered his head while flapping his ears.

"Okay, let's get a move on," said the head elephant, leading them down the slope in the direction of the Pinkerton. The animals stormed down the hillside, trampling everything in their path. They crashed through fences and stampeded through backyards. Nothing was spared, not even watermelon patches or flower gardens.

A quarter of the way down the hill, the rhino blundered through several rows of clotheslines. A white sheet that had been flapping in the breeze whisked across her face. She stopped for a moment to try and shake it off, but the wind kept the sheet over her head. As she continued down the hill she spun her body in circles till the wind finally blew the sheet off.

The rhino felt very uncomfortable in her heavy armor, with a horn hanging about her nose. It reminded her of a tree stump in her backyard. Before her mind had been put into this beast by the aliens, she was known by the local folk as, Sweet Pea, the town's pride and joy country music singer. She recently had a smash number one hit called, I'm a Diva Kingston Queen. People thought she had a real diva attitude because she never took no lip from anyone. As a rhino, she felt extraordinary powerful as if she could take on the whole world.

CHAPTER 20

Back on the steamboat, everyone's eyes shifted toward a group of animals heading up the road.

A moment later, the beasts made their way up to the base of the boarding ramp. The three Boe brother chimps climbed unnoticed across a rope tied to the bow of the boat, then swung up the face of the steamer to the upper levels.

Gorilla Mayor Jenkins walked up the boarding ramp carrying a two foot wide scroll. The moment he reached the passenger deck he stopped and let it roll down across of his hairy chest. In large letters it read, "I'm the mayor of Kingston. I'm not a hairy ape. The people in my town have been turned into animals by aliens. I'm dead serious. I'm not monkeying around. Please, I beg you, call the authorities for help!"

Everyone on board started to laugh out loud at the crazy sounding message. The next moment, Gorilla Mayor Jenkins waved for the rest of the animals to come aboard to help him out.

The zoo animals stampeded up the boarding ramp. The entire wedding party was now in a state of panic. Women jumped up from their seats and screamed, then pushed and shoved their way toward the bow of the boat, trying to get away from the wild looking animals.

The African elephant, Dr. Spencer, raised his trunk and blew it as loud as he could. "We're taking control of this boat! Every human must be thrown overboard!"

Gorilla Mayor Jenkins swung to the upper level where the Boe brothers had Captain Bremmer pinned face down on the wood deck. Mayor Jenkins picked up the captain's hat and placed it on his gorilla head.

Chimp Fred Boe looked up at the mayor and said, "What now… Captain… Mayor?

"There's only room for one captain on this here boat," said Gorilla Mayor Jenkins, raising Captain Bremmer's body over his head and taking him for a couple spins, before tossing him overboard. Some of the animals looked over the railing to see who made the big splash.

Every human crammed toward the bow of the boat. They pushed and squeezed in and around each other, trying to move forward, all the while looking back in horror as the animals slowly closed in.

Within a few short minutes, all the passengers jumped over the side rails and into the river.

After drifting downstream a couple minutes, the bride and groom, together with all the guests, swam ashore, then hurried back to their cars and sped off toward home.

CHAPTER 21

About ten minutes later, Holly and Charlie spotted the animals on the Pinkerton and headed up the boarding ramp to investigate.

"How can you tell which animal might be your parents?" said Charlie.

"If you want a direct answer, you have to ask a direct question." Holly boldly stepped up to each animal and said, "Mom… Dad?"

The orangutan looked at her, then slapped his forehead as if to say, You've got to be kidding.

Charlie tried to help out by asking the animals questions too. He peered down at Chimp Jim Boe and said, "Are you Holly's dad?"

Jim Boe jumped onto a wooden crate, then reached up and slapped Charlie across the face.

"This is harder work than I thought," said Charlie.

Holly's head slumped in disappointment. "I guess it could be safe to assume they're not here," she said, turning in a circle, looking at all the blank stares. "I know who you are, and what happened to you."

From the vantage point on top of Patricia the hippo's head, Kent spotted his brother, Charlie, standing at the opposite side of the deck. He squeaked as loud as he could to get his attention, but Charlie didn't hear or notice him as a mouse on the hippo's head.

Sweet Pea the rhino looked across at Holly and Charlie. "I really think they're here to help us," she said, tilting her head to one side.

The young elephant tapped the end of his trunk on top of their heads. "I saw these two," he said. "They were at the zoo!"

"He's right," said Gorilla Mayor Jenkins, looking down from the top deck, wearing his newly acquired captain's hat. "We can't take any chances! They might be aliens!"

"Sorry," said the elephant, swaying his head from side to side. He quickly wrapped his trunk around Holly and Charlie, then carried them to the side of the boat and dropped them into the river.

The animals peered over the railing a minute and watched them float downstream. Kent balanced himself on the highest vantage point—the tip of Patricia's ear. "Charlie, Charlie!" he squeaked as loud as he could, seeing his brother float away. He was worried because he knew his brother wasn't a great swimmer.

Holly and Charlie treaded water a ways downriver, then made it safely back to shore.

"I need to get back home to check on my parents and brother!" said Charlie.

Holly reached out and touched his muddied cheek. "Okay, but be careful. They may be—well, you know. If you ever see any eyes glow blue in the dark, get out fast. Keep safe. I'm going back to check with the twins to see if they found my parents and learned anything new."

They gave each other a big hug, and then headed back home.

CHAPTER 22

The night sky rumbled and bolted streaks of lightning as Charlie approached his residence. He stopped in the middle of the front lawn for a moment and stared at his home. Who left the lights on to every room? he thought. He rushed up the front steps and into the house. "Mom! Dad!" he called out.

Just inside the laundry room, the family dog, Puddles, was laying on her side with her front and back legs tied together with twine. A strip of white cotton cloth was wrapped around her head and mouth to keep her quiet.

"You'd better not try to make any noise, that is, if you know what's good for you!" said Helen, right before stepping out of the laundry room.

"Why, Charlie, you're sopping wet," said Helen, heading down the hallway. "We were worried sick about you. Where have you been?"

"Visiting my friend. Got caught up in the bad weather on the way back."

"Glad you're home safe, Son," said Burt. "That's quite a storm out there."

"I was worried about you also," said Charlie. "I thought you might have got stuck out in the storm somewhere—or worse. Where's Kent?"

"He's spending the night at his friend's house," said Helen. She glanced back down the hallway where she had Puddles tied up in the laundry room, then looked back at Charlie smiling.

"I need to get out of these wet clothes," said Charlie.

After heading upstairs and taking a shower, he entered his bedroom. He discovered his longhaired cat, Scooter, sound asleep on the top covers. Charlie turned the lights off and slipped into bed. A couple minutes later he heard the bedroom door start to creak open. His eyes bulged wide, seeing a hand slip inside and flip on the light switch.

"Who… who's there?"

Helen stepped inside and cast a big smile. "Just checking to make sure you're okay."

Charlie sighed. "Seriously, Mom, this is the first time I saw your hand creep into my bedroom to turn on the lights like that. Why aren't you wearing the emerald ring dad bought you? I've never seen you without it."

"You know, sweetheart, darling, I just… I just have it… in my bedroom… in the drawer."

Charlie's eyes narrowed, "Mom?" he said in a firm voice.

"Yes, sweetheart?"

He pointed his finger at her. "Dad never bought you that kind of ring. You don't have one!"

* * * * *

That moment, just inside the laundry room, Puddle tossed, turned and wiggled like crazy to try and get free. Tired and out of breath, she rested a moment. She gazed up toward the ironing board and noticed that the electric iron was left on. That gave her an idea on how she might possibly be able to get free. She wiggled onto the electric cord that ran along the floor, then started to roll back and forth on top of it. Each time she rolled on the cord it tugged and teetered the electric iron sitting on the ledge above, until, moments later, it came crashing to the floor right beside her. Puddles stretched the twine wrapped around her front feet toward the iron's hot edge. Smoke started to rise from the twine. Seconds later her front feet were set free. She quickly got her back legs into the same position and freed them also. But, as hard as she tried, she couldn't get the gag off from around her head and mouth.

Puddles tried to get out of the laundry room by pushing her head against the spring hinged door, but her feet kept sliding back across the hardwood floor. Looking back, she spotted a rubber floor mat. She gripped its edge in her teeth, then pulled it alongside the door. With the mat in place, she now had enough traction under her feet and was able to push the door open just enough to slip out.

She headed down the hallway and stopped just short of Burt's study room. Peeking around the corner, she saw him sitting in his chair reading a book. She darted by unnoticed and headed upstairs. At the top of the landing she suddenly stopped, hearing Helen and Charlie arguing in the bedroom. Puddles charged into Charlie's room right past Helen's feet and took a flying leap onto the bed. Scooter hissed and darted for the door, but Helen slammed it shut in front of him, blocking his way out.

Charlie couldn't believe his eyes! "What kind of monster would put a gag around Puddles head and mouth like this?" he shouted, squinting at Helen, "What the heck! Why is Puddles gagged?" Charlie quickly removed the cloth from around his head. "Are you trying to choke her or something?"

Helen smiled. "What kind of nonsense question is that?"

Charlie squinted at her. "Who are you, and why did you slam the door shut in front of Scooter like that?" He shook his head. "Can't you see he wants to get out?"

Helen laughed and swiped the air with her hand. "You ask too many silly questions."

"You're not my mom!" he said clenching his fists. "Where's my real mom?"

Helen smiled. "Why don't you ask your little doggie friend…Puddles."

Puddles slowly looked up at Charlie with tears in her eyes.

"No! No!" Charlie cried out. He leaned forward, peering into Puddle's face. "Mom?"

Puddles nodded. Charlie picked her up and held her eye level. "Mom… is it really you?"

Puddles nodded again.

Charlie leaned forward, squinting at Helen. "I want my mom back! Now!"

Helen reached over and switched off the light. Her eyes glowed blue. The closet door creaked open, and an alien stepped out. His entire body glowed in hues of blue. White sparks pulsated through his veins.

Puddles charged toward the intruder, but went right through the ghostly alien and crashed headfirst into the closet door. She stumbled about a moment, looking dizzy, then shook her head to clear her vision.

The alien flashed a light beam at Charlie causing him to slump back onto the bed, then turned into a vapor and floated directly over Charlie. He tried to pass into his body, but was unable to do so.

"He's protected!" said the alien, looking very upset. Without saying another word he disappeared through the wall.

Helen looked startled and angry.

Charlie leaned up in bed and tried to clear his head, as Helen reached out and grabbed his arm. "How… how did you get the powder?" She moved her face up to his, and said, "Who's been helping you?"

When Puddles saw Helen the alien start to shake Charlie, she charged straight ahead and sunk her teeth into her leg. Helen released Charlie and stumbled to the floor in pain.

Charlie, Puddles and Scooter made a run for it out the door and down the hallway.

"Charlie," said Burt, staring up at them from the base of the stairs, blocking their way out. "What's the big hurry? Did something frighten you, Puddles and Scooter?"

"Where's my real dad?" said Charlie, squinting down at him from half way up the stairs.

Burt grinned and laughed. "Well, if you must know, he turned into a big ape, and is hanging out with all the other hairy animals."

Helen limped down the hallway with an evil frown glued to her face. "I'm going to get you. Come here, you little mutt!"

Puddles shifted her attention from Helen to Burt, then, without a moment's hesitation, charged down the steps right past Charlie. On the sixth step from the bottom, she took a flying leap with her mouth stretched open and landed her choppers right between Burt's legs. He let out a loud howl, stumbling to the floor in pain.

Charlie and Scooter raced down the stairs right past Burt, then darted out the front door with Puddles leading the way.

CHAPTER 23

Holly paced back and forth across the mansion's attic floor, pondering her next plan of action, when, all of a sudden, she saw a pebble bounce off against the windowpane. She raised the window and stared down toward the grounds below. "Oh my gosh!" she said, seeing Charlie and Puddles staring back up at her through the sheets of rain.

Holly stuck her head out the window and called out, "Charlie! Quick! Hide!… Get behind the hedge. I'll be right down."

He followed her instructions and ducked behind some shrubbery.

Moments later, Charlie saw Holly open the cellar window and wave him over. He handed Puddles through the opening first, then squeezed inside through the cellar opening.

"Careful," he said. "That's my mom."

"What?" said Holly, thinking she must have misunderstood.

"It's my mom. I'm dead serious."

Holly held Puddles eye-level. "Mrs. Robinson?"

Puddles nodded.

Holly looked shocked. "Oh… my… gosh." She looked over at Charlie. "Is you mom a d-o-g?"

Tears started to trickle down Puddles face.

"Please, don't, you know… say…"

"Yes, of course. I'm terribly sorry, Puddles… I mean… Mrs. Robinson," she said, giving her the most sorrowful look she could.

Charlie followed Holly's lead past the secret wall of crates and up the spiraling stone stairway. Instead of a cold wind bearing down on them, they were greeted with a warm breeze that blew against their backs, beginning at the first step up. It was as if they were being urged forward by something or someone.

Holly stepped into the attic and looked back at Charlie. "Sorry about your mom."

Charlie sighed. "We need to find a way to get our families and everyone else back to normal… fast."

Holly pointed toward the lantern sitting on the windowsill. "That's where I met them."

"Who?"

"You know; the twins, Stephanie and Agatha."

"Oh, yes," he said nodding. "The ghosts. How could have I forgotten."

Holly stepped up to the lantern and peered at the wick inside. "This is how we know when they're coming. When the light starts to glow inside."

Charlie' eyes widened. "You mean it lights up all by itself?" His attention was suddenly drawn to the lump on the bottom bunk. "Uh… what's under that blanket?" he said, stepping back.

"Calcium—a whole lot of calcium." She stepped between Charlie and the bed. "Calcium is good for everyone's bones."

"Calcium? Did you say? As in bones?" He peered over her shoulder.

Just then, a flicker of light sparked in the lantern. Charlie watched the flame grow larger and brighter by the second, until the shadows in the room faded away.

Agatha and Stephanie floated in through the back door and passed right through Charlie. They stopped next to the lantern, then turned and faced Holly and Charlie with smiles on their faces.

"Stephanie… Agatha," said Holly. "I would like you to meet my close friend Charlie, and his mom, who has been taken over, and now is Puddles the pug."

Puddles smiled.

"Oh, Miss Holly, pudgy Puddles looks so

adorable!" said Stephanie, "A creamy marshmallow face. So sweet."

"Yes marshmallow… yummy marshmallow." said Agatha.

The twins walked up to Charlie, then reached out to shake his hand, but he just stood there with his arms limp at his side, looking as if he was in a trance.

Holly flashed her hand up and down in front of Charlie's face, and snapped her fingers, but didn't get a response.

The twins looked curiously at Charlie, not quite sure what his problem was. They leaned to their left and right, staring at him from either side, then glanced back at each other.

Stephanie glanced over at Holly. "Do you think he likes us?"

Agatha turned a little bit sad looking. "Do you think he'll be our friend… our friend?"

Holly grinned. "Why, of course he'll be your friend." She snapped her fingers in front of his face again. "Charlie! Come on… snap out of it."

He blinked, finding it hard to believe seeing two ghostly figures standing in before him.

Holly placed her hand onto his shoulder. "They're here to help us. Well?"

"Well what?"

"Aren't you going to at least shake their hands?"

"Of course. How rude of me." He reached out,

extending his hand too far, and it passed through Stephanie's waist. "Sorry."

The twins smiled and gave Charlie ghostly hugs.

"Miss Holly," said Stephanie, eyes stretched wide. "We have terrible news!"

"Yes terrible… terrible!" said Agatha.

"Miss Holly," said Stephanie, "Bellarouse's neighbors are all pigs now," said Stephanie, casting a sad countenance.

"Yes, pigs… pigs," said Agatha, head sinking low.

Charlie clenched his hand into a fist. "The Druskys? Pigs?" he said turning toward Holly. "We have to take action. We can't just stay here and do nothing!"

Holly nodded in agreement. "But, how to save them? The only thing I can think of this moment is for us to try and set them free."

Charlie nodded. "Good plan. We'll just have to take a chance on getting caught. We'd best do it early morning, before daybreak."

Holly looked over at the twins. "Did you learn anything else? Anything that could help us save our parents, the town… the planet?" The twins stared at each other for a moment, then looked back at them with blank stares.

"We're sorry, Miss Holly. Nothing new… not yet."

"Nothing new… not yet. Not yet," said Agatha.

"However," said Stephanie, "we do know they're planning to attack the town of Claremont next. The aliens told Bellarouse there aren't enough pets to put all the human minds into."

"They have a new weapon they're planning to use, yes… use," said Agatha.

Holly's eyes bulged wide. "Weapon? What kind of weapon?"

Stephanie stepped closer. "Miss Holly, we don't know what it is yet. As soon as we learn more, we will come again to let you know."

Agatha stepped alongside her sister. "Yes, come… come."

"What if we can't get back here?" said Holly.

Stephanie reached out and placed her hand on her shoulder. "Miss Holly, when we have news, we will find you. We will come."

Agatha placed her hand on Charlie's shoulder. "Yes, we will find you… find you."

Holly and Charlie thanked the twins and waved then goodbye.

The twins disappeared through the wall, and the lantern's light faded to a flicker before going out completely.

CHAPTER 24

Charlie and Holly approached the Drusky Farm under the cover of darkness. When they neared the barn they heard frogs croaking by the water's edge, then silence, followed by the sound of several splashes. A large rooster perched on an overhead branch flapped its red comb to one side, keeping a watchful eye on the two strangers.

"I'm going to set Button Rouge free first," said Holly, whispering into Charlie's ear as they neared the barn. "Perhaps he can lead us to the rest of his family."

"Good idea. While you're doing that I'll start from the back of the barn and work my way toward the front."

The moment they entered the barn, they heard the sounds of pigs' feet rustling to-and-fro.

Toward the back of the barn, the Drusky family

turned pigs; Frank, Annabel, Lance, and Meagan, scurried to the front of their pen to see who was coming.

The moment Holly walked up to Button's pen she was startled by the sound of a squeaky man's voice calling down to her from the hayloft. "Who's there?" said the man, "Who's down there?" he repeated.

Holly squinted toward the hayloft, trying to see where the voice was coming from. She was so nervous she could feel her heart pounding in her chest.

A light flashed down into her face. "Are you a pig-napper?"

"No, Sir. My name is, Holly." She looked up, trying so see who it was through the glare. "Are you the pig night watchman?" She motioned with her hands for Charlie to stay out of sight, beneath the loft.

"What are you doing with your hands?" shouted the man. "Keep them still!"

Holly watched a stubby man step down the ladder, then grab a pitchfork. His beach-ball belly bounced up and down between his blue jeans suspenders as he walked up to her. She looked down into his squinty eyes and thought, this guy must have been the runt of the litter.

He stared up at Holly with squinted eyes. "What's you doing in here?"

"I heard you have some really sweet pigs, and I thought I'd swing on by and check 'em out."

"You know what I think?" said Stubby, placing one hand firmly on his hip.

"What?" she replied, placing her hand on her hip too.

Stubby stretched his neck out toward Holly. "I think you be a pig poacher!" He poked her left shoulder with his index finger. "That's what I think you be! A Missy poacher!"

"That's ridiculous." Holly chuckled. "I hate poached pig."

"Smarty pants lady. Huh. Well…we'll let's see what Mr. Drusky has to say about this." He turned and headed for the barn door.

Charlie suddenly burst out from the shadows and tackled Mr. Stubby to the ground.

"Quick! Find something to tie him up!" said Charlie. "Hurry!"

Holly handed him a roll of tape she found hanging on a wooden peg.

They quickly put tape over his mouth, then secured his arms and legs.

Charlie looked over at Holly. "Help me drag him behind this bale of hay."

With the man safely concealed and gagged, Holly stepped over to Button Rouge's pen and set him free.

Button immediately took off running as fast as

his four legs could carry him toward the back of the barn where the rest of his family was caged.

"Hey, it looks like he might have led us to them!" said Charlie.

The instant Charlie unlatched the pen, Annabel raced out and kissed Albert, with the rest of the family snuggling around him.

"Looks like they're happy to be reunited, even as pigs." He knelt down and put his face a foot away from the pigs. "Mr. Drusky? Mrs. Drusky?" Charlie whispered. "Is that you?"

Annabel responded by nodding. Frank nodded as well.

"Lance? Meagan?" Holly whispered. Two smaller pigs scurried up to her and nodded.

"We found them all right," said Holly.

"What next?" said Charlie.

"Let's free all the pigs. That way it will be harder for the aliens to try and catch them."

"Good idea. Let's do it."

Holly and Charlie wasted no time in unlatching all the pens.

Frank Drusky was the biggest hog of all, and all the other pigs looked up to him and followed his lead out of the barn.

* * * * *

Holly and Charlie decided to head back toward

the McGuire Mansion by way of the back roads to keep out of sight. Along the way they came across the Kingston Cemetery.

Charlie took a deep breath, "We have to cross it to get back home."

Holly noticed that as far as she could see every plot of ground was occupied. She was surprised at the sheer number of gravestones that lay before her. "This must have been a popular place to retire," said Holly.

"Right, Kingston is an old, tightly knit community going back to Pre-Civil War time."

A light breeze rolled in a creepy ground-hugging layer of fog, about a foot thick.

Charlie suddenly stopped and peered down at a large headstone having the name, Melvin Cobb Sr., chiseled into the black marble. "That's Uncle Melvin's dad's grave," he said, looking back at Holly.

Charlie looked down at the vase in front of the headstone filled with flowers; not store bought ones, but wild ones you might expect to find growing around the surrounding countryside: brambling pink roses, daisies, and leafy green foliage.

"That's weird," said Charlie. "The only one who ever brought him fresh flowers was his son, my Uncle Melvin—and he's been missing for some time now."

Holly was about to pick a wildflower out of the vase, when she heard a loud growl sound out from beneath the blanket of fog at the base of the headstone.

She quickly stepped back. "What was that!"

Another ear-piercing screech sounded. A huge black cat leaped out from the fog and landed on top of Melvin Cobb Sr.'s headstone.

"Nightmare!" said Charlie. "It's Nightmare!"

The cat aimed his glowing eyes at Holly, then, without warning, took a flying leap onto her shoulder. It screeched into her ear with his back arched, fur standing on end. Holly jumped and twisted about. "Get him off! Help me, Charlie! Get him off!"

Charlie ran up behind and flung Nightmare to the ground. The cat darted off beneath the blanket of fog.

"How creepy was that!" she said, trying to catch her breath, "I wonder if Nightmare got mad because I tried to take one of those flowers?"

"Who knows," said Charlie, "I don't know what's got into that cat lately. He's been acting crazy ever since Melvin disappeared!"

At The Break of Dawn

Back at the Drusky farm, Frank the alien reached over the edge of the bed to answer the phone. "Hello?" he said in a sleepy voice.

"Hey there, Frank, it's Mickey at Bernie's Ham-

It-Up. You okay? You don't sound like your normal self."

He yawned. "Sure. Just waking up."

"Just waking up!" said Mickey, raising his voice. "You got the flu or something? Say, just called to confirm the pickup this morning."

"Pickup?"

"Are you sure you're okay? The pigs. You do have the pigs? Don't you?"

"Yeah, sure, right."

"I'll be there with my truck within the hour."

* * * * *

Alien Annabel Drusky flipped eggs in a grease-sputtering skillet for her new family. They were still trying to get accustomed to living in their new bodies.

A short time later, Mickey drove his Ham-It-Up truck onto the Drusky farm lot and pressed his horn to announce his arrival. Instead of making a honking noise, the truck made loud hog squeals.

Annabel peered out through the kitchen blinds and saw the truck. A couple minutes later, Mickey still didn't see anyone coming out, so he pressed his horn again—harder this time. Instead of squeals, the truck's horn made loud grunt noises.

"Just a minute!" said Alien Frank, hopping out the back door on one foot while trying to get his other boot on. He waved for Mickey to start backing his truck up to the barn. When Frank opened the door his mouth dropped open in shock. There wasn't a pig in sight. He couldn't believe his eyes.

Frank heard the truck pull up behind him, followed by Mickey's voice. "Where's my pigs?" he shouted. "You better not have made me drive clear out here for nothin'!" he blared.

Frank stepped into the barn and found his farmhand tied up behind one of the bales of hay with his mouth taped shut.

Frank quickly removed the tape from his mouth. "Buford, what happened?"

"I was jumped! It was a tall guy with baggy jeans and blue striped shirt. He had a girl with him too—reddish, shoulder-length hair."

Frank shook his head. "You let a couple kids steal my pigs?"

"I'm sorry boss. The guy was really sneaky. Jumped out of the shadows he did! Got me from behind."

"They couldn't have gotten far," said Frank. "We'll get the pigs back."

"Well just fine," said Mickey, "but hurry...don't be takin' too long about that."

Frank ran into the house and made a call to Alien Sheriff Gary. He told him what had happened and gave a description of the two pig-nappers. Shortly thereafter, a posse of sixty alien town folk started to scour the surrounding countryside in search of the missing animals and pig-nappers.

* * * * *

An hour later, on the other side of town, Holly and Charlie finally made it back to the McGuire mansion. Holly tried to open the cellar window, but it wouldn't budge. "That's strange," she said. "I'm sure I left it unlocked."

While Charlie tried to pry it open, someone suddenly grabbed his shoulder from behind. It was Alien Sheriff Gary! And he had a dozen alien-folk with him too!

"Did you really think you could outsmart me?" said Sheriff Gary.

Holly and Charlie were promptly dragged across the lawn and ushered into the back of the patrol car.

"My mom?" said Charlie, whispering into Holly's ear. "I have to get back to the attic and make sure she's all right."

Holly placed her hand on his arm and whispered, "The twins. I'm sure they'll take care of her till we get back."

Sergeant Rex, the bloodhound, jumped into the car and stared back at them from the passenger front seat.

"Sheriff Gary?" said Charlie, to the dog, figuring

that the sheriff's mind was now in the bloodhound. "Is that you?"

Sergeant Rex nodded.

Alien Sheriff Gary received a call on his way to the jailhouse notifying him that the missing pigs had been spotted traveling east along Roger's Pass. He sent out an all point bulletin alert. Within minutes, a caravan of thirty cars and trucks sped out to capture the runaway pigs.

Minutes later, Holly and Charlie found themselves whisked out of the patrol car and quickly put behind bars.

"There now, that ought to hold you two," said Sheriff Gary, locking their cell. "We'll be getting back soon enough to take care of you two. First, I need to help round up some pigs."

Sergeant Rex sat next to the cell, and flopped his head side-to-side, exchanging glances between Charlie, Holly and keys hanging on the wall.

"Rex!" said the Sheriff. "Don't you be getting any ideas now about those keys!"

Charlie looked through the bars at Rex. "It's OK. We'll be all right."

"Come here!" said Sheriff Gary as he headed for the front door.

Rex stayed by the cell.

"Sure bet you're coming with me, dog," said the sheriff, looking more irritated. "Now, come over here!" he repeated. "I don't trust you."

Rex just sat there, refusing to leave Charlie and Holly by themselves.

"I said come… Dog! Now!" said Sheriff Gary, raising his voice.

Charlie looked down at Rex. "You'd better go. We'll be okay."

The moment Rex exited the front door, Sheriff Gary switched off the lights, leaving them alone in the dark.

* * * * *

About forty minutes later, Stephanie and Agatha, surprised them by suddenly appearing through the side wall.

"What a relief to see you here!" said Holly.

Stephanie giggled. "Miss Holly, Sir Charlie, glad to see you are not harmed."

Agatha quickly retrieved the keys and unlocked their cell.

"Is my mom, Puddles, OK?" asked Charlie with a worried look. "I couldn't get to her."

Agatha reached out and put her hand on Charlie's shoulder. "Yes. She's OK, OK."

"We'll make sure she's taken good care of till you can get back," said Stephanie. "Try not to worry."

"Thanks so much," said Charlie.

"Miss Holly… we spied Bellarouse's house."

"Yes, her house… her house," said Agatha.

"Miss Holly, we learned that there are not enough animals in Claremont to put the human minds into. They plan to use something new. They plan to put it in free drinks—for everyone at the circus."

"Yes... free! Everyone...everyone! At the circus," said Agatha.

"At the end of the circus, everyone will turn into animals according to their personalities," said Stephanie.

"We can't let this happen," said Holly. "We got to stop it; trip them up."

"Miss Holly, we learned that a tall clown will do it. They call him, Mr. Green Wig. He will be there an hour before the circus starts and put the powder inside the barrels of drinks."

"We have to be there to stop him!" said Charlie.

Holly stepped over to Sheriff Gary's desk. "Let's take a look around to see if we can find anything useful to capture Mr. Green Wig." After looking through the desk drawers, her eyes suddenly lit up. "Nice! This might make him laugh—till his eyes water," she said, holding up a can of pepper spray.

Charlie found a pair of shiny handcuffs. "Cool! Look at these. This should help out."

"Good find, Charlie. That will come in handy in case we have to give him a restraining order."

Stephanie stepped up to Holly. "Be careful when you find the new alien powder. We overheard

Bellarouse warn her daughter—never so much as to even touch it. You see, Miss Holly, if even a tiny amount of this were to be swallowed by someone already protected by the other powder, the results would be horrible. True, they would not turn into an animal, but whatever you are inside—good or evil—will be multiplied hundreds, if not thousands of times."

"Yes, yes," said Agatha, "Hundreds, thousands of times."

"Perhaps we can think of a way of harnessing this power against the aliens," said Holly.

"Any ideas?" said Charlie.

"We all know Bellarouse's daughter is an evil child. What if we purposely found a way to get her to eat a large amount of this substance all at once?"

"Didn't Stephanie just say…"

"Yes. She would probably become thousands of times more evil powerful," said Holly.

"How will that help get rid of the aliens?" said Charlie.

"If we could possibly turn her evilness against them…"

"It's a long shot. But who knows," said Charlie. "How about getting Marie back to normal afterwards?"

"What's normal for her?"

"You've got a point. Perhaps it might wear off."

"We'll tackle that problem when it comes. We

need to concentrate on getting the aliens to leave this planet any way we can." She looked back at the twins. "Think—this is important, did you overhear where Bellarouse and her daughter Marie might be planning to go next?"

"The circus, Miss Holly."

"Yes, yes, the circus, in Claremont, this morning… this morning," said Agatha.

"We overheard Marie threaten to tear the circus apart if she didn't get what she wanted," said Stephanie. "Bellarouse promised to give her two cases of strawberry yogurt at intermission time, Miss Holly; in a separate tent, by the main circus."

"Yes, yes, and she will be entertained by two hired clowns… clowns," said Agatha. "To keep her happy, happy."

"Perfect," said Holly. "Now I need your help. Charlie and I need to be those two clowns."

"What?" said Charlie, with a chuckle.

Holly faced the twins. "We need you to scare off those clowns so we can take their place and go undercover. We're going to spike her yogurt before she gets there."

The twins' faces glowed with courage.

"Miss Holly, I think… I know we can help," said Stephanie.

"Yes, we can do it… We can. We can!" said Agatha, clenching her fist.

Holly admired their toughness and willpower.

The twins waved goodbye, then vanished before their eyes.Holly and Charlie left the jail and headed toward the Claremont Circus to try and stop Mr. Green Wig, and play the part of a couple clowns in order to get the chance to spike Marie's yogurt with the alien powder

.

CHAPTER 25

The moment Holly and Charlie entered the Claremont circus tent they saw four trapeze artists dressed in white leotards practicing their swinging acrobatics seventy feet above the ground. In the show ring below, they were delighted to see four miniature poodles with rainbow-colored ribbons tied to their pom-pom hair jump up and down to the beat of rumba music and take turns hopping over a pole held at each end by brightly dressed clowns. Heading toward the back of the tent, they observed six men on ladders decorating the circus elephants with feathered headdresses and glittering tassels.

The moment Holly stepped out of the tent her

eyes stretched wide. "There! There he is!" she said, spotting Mr. Green Wig. He was carrying a sealed canister filled with alien powder and heading across the back circus lot! Holly thought the clown looked so tall he might be walking on stilts.

Charlie and Holly followed Mr. Green Wig to one of the trailers and took a peek inside. They saw Mr. Green Wig head toward eight, fifty-five gallon refreshment drums against the far wall.

Holly boldly ran up to Mr. Green Wig and tapped him on the shoulder from behind just as he was about to put some of the alien powder into one of drums filled with orange soda.

"Hold it right there!" she said, squinting up into his rainbow painted eyes. "You even look at me funny, Mr. Green Hairdo, and my friend Macy here will make you cry!"

The clown looked over at Charlie. "Is that Macy?" he said with a laugh. "Gosh! I'm scared," he said, laughing some more.

"He's not Macy, funny clown," said Holly laughing back at him.

Mr. Green Wig looked a bit confused not knowing what she was talking about.

"People on the street know Macy by his real name. It's Mr. Mace, clown! He can make anybody cry. I'll show you how!" Right then, she flashed up her can of mace containing pepper spray, and let him have a generous dose right between the eyes.

Mr. Green Wig suddenly started to cry so hard he could hardly contain himself. Charlie stuck his foot out in front of the big crybaby and gave him a funny trip. After stumbling like a twiggy tree to the floor, his eyes watered so hard he was making boo-hoo tears all over the floor. It was really a sight to behold.

Charlie wrestled the clown's hands behind him, gave him a restraining order, then slapped on the shiny metal cuffs around his wrists. Holly helped out by slipping off the clown's belt and using it to tie his ankles together. Charlie removed Mr. Green Wig's polka dot silk hankie from his breast pocket and used it as a gag to keep him from laughing out loud. Next, they grabbed his arms and legs and dragged Mr. Green Wig into the storage closet. Holly placed the canister filled with the alien powder in a leather bag strapped to her waist.

* * * * *

There were twelve trailers parked on a grassy area just off a dirt road behind the main circus tent. Two circus folks, a man and woman in their thirties, stepped out of the third trailer from the end dressed in red-and-yellow polka-dot clown costumes. They started doing stretching exercises on a grassy area just outside their trailer

"Can you believe it?" said Lester, the male

clown. "Us having to give a private performance for some brat named Marie from Kingston!"

"Sure, sure, but it's just a one-time gig," said Anaya. "Get over it. You're good at laughing things off."

The two clowns stepped back into their trailer to finish putting on their makeup before the start of their performance. They sat in private dressing rooms in the same trailer, each having large mirrors, brightly lit by six baseball-sized bulbs strung across the top. A half dozen wigs and several polyester clown suits hung in each tiny dressing room. The floors of the rooms were cluttered with several pairs of oversized, brightly colored clown shoes.

As Anaya started to powder her face with a base of white makeup, Stephanie's image suddenly appeared within the mirror directly in front of her.

"Mirror, mirror, on the wall," said Stephanie, looking cross-eyed, twisting the corners of her mouth in opposite directions with all her front teeth and gums showing. "Who's the funniest of them all?"

Anaya stared stone-faced into the mirror, eyes stretched wide, jaw hanging open in shock.

"Boo!" shouted Stephanie at the top of her lungs, waving her hands wildly above her head.

That same moment, in the next dressing room, Agatha appeared in the mirror before Lester.

"Mirror, mirror on the wall, who's the craziest

of them all?" said Agatha, rolling her eyes and pushing her nose back to make herself look like a pig, exposing her front teeth.

Lester squinted and blinked, moving his face closer to the mirror to see if the image was some kind of mirage. That moment, Agatha let loose a hysterical laugh that rippled her image in the mirror, giving her a twisted, warped look.

Anaya and Lester jumped up from their seats, toppled back in their chairs, then made mad dashes out of their booths. They collided ungracefully in the hallway, stumbled to the floor, then quickly scrambled back to their feet and sprinted out of the trailer.

"Hey, look at that!" said Holly pointing out to Charlie two clowns running down the road as fast as they could.

Stephanie and Agatha passed through a large tree where Holly and Charlie were hiding behind, then turned and faced them.

"Miss Holly. We did it," said Stephanie, giving a warm smile, pointing at the third trailer from the end.

Agatha raised her arm and pointed too. "Yes, did it... did it!"

"Were those the two clowns who were supposed to serve Marie her special yogurt, during intermission?" said Holly.

The twins nodded.

"Great!" said Holly.

"Seriously, thanks so much!" said Charlie.

"Good luck," said Stephanie, embracing Charlie.

"Yes, good luck… luck," said Agatha, giving Holly a hug.

"We must try and help the Druskys now, Miss Holly," said Stephanie.

"Yes, help… help," Agatha echoed.

The twins waved goodbye and vanished before their eyes.

Holly looked around the side of the tree and saw that the coast was clear. "Okay, let's do it," she said, grabbing Charlie's hand, before running together across the grass and into the trailer. Heading down the narrow hallway, each one entered separate dressing rooms. Holly applied a base of white makeup to her face, followed by a sweeping red and purple painted smile. She added some decorative yellow dots to her face for good measure, then zipped her body into a white clown suit patterned with red balloon images. "Great!" she said, finding a pair of red clown shoes to slip into. Next, she put on a blond wig that billowed ten inches above her head, swooped down, then up again in a giant wave. As a finishing touch, she added a large tomato nose that squeaked when pinched or pushed.

She stepped out of her dressing room at the same time Charlie stepped out of his. They faced each other and got a good laugh. Charlie had on a white outfit with purple dots, complimented by a big red wig. His face was covered with white makeup. He painted on a big red smile and found a purple ball to stick over his nose.

"Why, I haven't seen you look so happy like this before," said Charlie, "That clown outfit of yours reminds me of the song, Happy Days Are Here Again."

"I wish I felt like happy days are here again, Charlie the Clown."

Charlie stepped up to Holly and squeezed her tomato nose, making a loud squeak. "Nice choice. If I'm driving a car and someone gets in my way I can squeeze your nose to get their attention."

Holly made her nose honk, "Like this." She chuckled. "You're a natural clown, Charlie, makeup or not."

Holly tripped over her red clown shoes on the way out of the trailer, falling face down onto the grass.

"Careful Big Foot," said Charlie helping her back up, "You need to save your funny moments for the circus guests."

"OK, Smarty Clown."

Holly and Charlie entered the main circus tent through the back stage area. They saw a slow-moving tide of men, women, and children of all ages flowing down the aisles, quickly filling the seats.

"I don't think I can do this. I don't think I can

fill these clown shoes," said Charlie, feeling his body start to freeze up.

"Perhaps instead of stage fright, you're getting clown fright." Holly reached out and put her hand on his shoulder. "Don't pout. Just relax and clown around with me." She handed him one of the clown's props—a bucket filled with shredded bits of paper. Take this and play cat and mouse. Try and get me."

"I'll do my best, but I don't know if I can get anyone to laugh out loud."

Charlie pretended to chase Holly around the arena in front the first row of spectators. Each time she stopped and looked back, she noticed that Charlie was closer to her than he'd been the time before. He just stood there, with the bucket at his side, pretending to look up at the ceiling. The fourth time she stopped, Charlie was right behind her. He raised his bucket over her head and poured the contents on top of her clown wig. Paper confetti fluttered all over Holly and a mother holding her daughter. Her six-year-old son received a big dose of paper too. The young girl burst out crying.

The mother tried to comfort her daughter as she brushed bits of paper out of her hair. "Look what you did. You, awful, awful clown!"

Charlie, stepped up to Holly and whispered into her ear, "You have to redeem yourself. Make the girl laugh! Come on! Do it Holly. Do it!"

Holly pointed at herself. "Me? I'm not the one

who threw the paper, but since you have a touch of clown fright, I'll try and play the part of the funniest clown." She took a deep breath and looked back into the girl's pouting face. "I can do this," she said, whispering to herself. She found a peanut in her pocket and held it up to the girl's face. "Baby want a peanut?" she said in a high, squeaky voice.

Charlie rolled his eyes. "You've got to be kidding. You're so bad!"

The girl started crying again, then suddenly threw her fist squarely into Holly's clown nose, making a loud squeak.

"Ouch," said Holly, feeling her real nose beneath the fake one get squashed. Just for the heck of it, she reached up and squeaked her nose again. The girl stopped crying and started to laugh.

"Oh, you like that? You like my tomato nose, do you?" Holly tried to think of something else to get her to laugh. "It's a nice vegetable day, isn't it? You eat your broccoli, like a good girl, don't you?" she said, sticking her big tomato nose in front of the girl.

To Holly's disappointment, the girl started to pout, then burst out crying again.

"How about I stick a tomato up your nose!" said the mother, shoving Holly back, causing her to fall back to the ground. The mother leaned forward, then pointed and laughed at her. "You're revolting!" she said. The whole family slapped their knees, laughed and pointed at her.

"Gremlins," said Holly, whispering to herself. She got up and brushed sawdust off her costume.

"Look," said Charlie. "You're a five-star clown!" He pointed to a crowd of people pointing and laughing at her.

Outwardly, Holly continued to clown around, but on the inside, she felt like venting her true feelings toward the mother. She thought about pushing a whipped cream pie into the lady's face, then rotating it to the left, right, then the left again as if she was pretending to open a safe, but lost the combination, and had to try it over and over again.

"Ut-Oh," whispered Charlie, catching sight of Bellarouse and her daughter Marie heading down the main aisle. He looked over at Holly. "Do you think they'll recognize us?"

Holly placed her hand on his shoulder. "In these costumes? With our fake hair and funny noses? Don't worry Charlie. She'll never guess who we are, especially from way up in those seats."

* * * * *

Opening day at the circus had drawn a crowd of over two thousand men, women, and children. The music swelled as the ringmaster entered the arena. He tipped his black top hat before a sea of popcorn-chomping, peanut-cracking, soda-guzzling spectators and said, "Ladies and gentleman, welcome to the Big Top Circus Extravaganza!"

Right after his announcement, elephants and circus entertainers started to parade around the arena.

CHAPTER 26

Holly and Charlie, still dressed in clown disguises, made a quick exit out of the main tent and ran across an open field toward a smaller guest tent reserved for Marie and her mother.

"Oh no!" said Holly staring into the tent. She saw an empty table at the center with two chairs tied with red and yellow balloons. "It's almost time for her to be here and the two cases of yogurt are nowhere in sight."

Charlie checked his watch. "I wonder why it wasn't delivered yet?"

Only twenty minutes remained before circus intermission time—and Marie's expected arrival.

Charlie and Holly stood by the tent entrance and peered out across the circus grounds. Minutes later, a white truck appeared down the road, heading their way fast. The driver pulled up alongside and said, "Hey... you two clowns! Are you the ones I'm supposed to deliver these two cases of yogurt to?"

"Yep, that's a big happy clown face yes," said Holly, faking a big laugh. She took the metal clipboard from the driver and signed the receipt. "You may just have saved the lives of everyone in town, and possibly even the whole world!"

"What, for strawberry yogurt? Get real clown!" said the driver. He got back into his truck and drove off with a big smile glued to his face.

"Hurry," said Holly, looking over at Charlie. "Let's get everything set up inside before she comes." She quickly removed the sealed canister of alien powder from the leather pouch she'd hidden under her clown pants. "We only have a few minutes left to spike the yogurt with this extraterrestrial powder. Let's hope and pray it doesn't have any weird taste or our Kingston princess brat won't touch it."

Before opening the container, Holly and Charlie put on rubber gloves and white cotton masks they had stashed in their back pockets. Holly tried to keep her hand steady as she carefully portioned out one teaspoon of alien powder for each container of yogurt. Charlie mixed it together, then replaced the lids. Holly was brimming with hope, whereas Charlie was banking on her plan, hoping it wouldn't go bust.

"Be careful," said Charlie, noticing Holly's hands start to shake as she added another teaspoon of alien powder.

"Yes, Mr. Gourmet Clown. Be sure not to lick

your smile too… strawberry smarty."

Charlie gave Holly a light tap on her shoulder. "I still don't understand how getting her to eat all this is going to help get rid of the aliens."

"If what the twins told us about the powder is true, and Marie gets a thousand or so doses of it all at once, then quite possibly her sugar-and-spice and not everything-is-so-nice personality could mushroom into something… well, let's say, quite distasteful for the aliens—and unfortunately for us as well. But that's a chance we'll have to take."

Charlie kept a lookout by the tent door for any signs of Bellarouse and Marie.

A short time later he looked back at Holly, "They're coming! I see them! They're on their way… now!"

Holly glanced out of the tent for a look-see. "That's them all right."

Charlie's hands started to twitch nervously. "Won't they, like, figure us out?"

"Your face, no. Your voice, maybe. Remember— think mime."

"What?"

"Mime… mute. Communicate with your hands. You're good at charades, aren't you?"

"Oh, yeah, right. Easy for you to say, Emmy-winning clown."

"Let me do the jabbering. I'll cloak my voice in mystery," she said.

"You are a mystery."

Holly and Charlie stood at opposite ends of the yogurt table and practiced making funny clown moves as they waited for the star appearance of Bellarouse and Marie.

Bellarouse waved and bowed before for her daughter as she entered the tent, treating her like she was a real princess. "There's your special yogurt and clowns my sweet cupcake; just as I promised."

"I… I don't like being called food! I told you that!" said Marie, stomping into the tent right past her mother. She suddenly stopped halfway between the door and the table of yogurt, then squinted back and forth between the two clowns. "I wanted creepy clowns," she snarled, snapping her head back, squinting at her mother. "I told you that, Mom! I wanted creepy clowns! These are happy clowns." She snarled loudly. "I think they're awful looking."

"But, sweet angel cake, give them a chance," said Bellarouse, palms stretched out toward the two entertainers.

Charlie could tell by Bellarouse's facial expression that she was busy thinking… trying to figure out who the mystery clowns were beneath the costumes, fake hair, and thick makeup. Even with his disguise, Charlie was worried that he might do something to give away his true self and spoil their whole plan.

Marie didn't seem to pay any attention to the

girl clown. Her focus was drawn entirely to the boy clown who was holding a cup of yogurt for her with a giant smile painted on his face.

Holly remembered how she made people laugh in the circus. She stepped up to Marie, then leaned forward and whispered into her ear. "Tap my nose and I'll squeak. You like rodents… don't you?" said Holly in a silly voice.

Charlie shook his head, and rolled his eyes in disbelief at the stupid remark, but, to his utter amazement, Marie's stone face slowly started to crack into a smile.

"Rats," said Marie. "I like rats. Rats squeak." She looked back at her mom. "I want to squeak this clown's nose like a giant rat. I want to squeak it now!"

Bellarouse sported a big smile, then nodded. "Go ahead my sweet. Make it squeak."

Marie looked back at Holly, then reached out and repeatedly squeaked her nose with light taps. "These are little rats," said Marie, smiling. "I like big rats. Big ones, I tell you!" With that said, she coiled her hand into a tight fist and let Holly have it with a strong blow to her nose. Holly heard a giant squeak, then blacked out and fell flat on her back. When she came too after a couple of seconds, she saw Marie standing over her laughing and giggling.

Seeing Holly get punched like that and lying helpless on the ground made Charlie's face flush red beneath his white makeup.

Holly quickly got back up and gestured with her hands for Charlie to stay cool.

Charlie felt like blowing his wig and lashing out right then and there, but remained silent like a true mime.

Marie shifted her attention toward her special treat.

"Strawberry fields forever for you, rat squeaker," said Holly, exchanging glances between Marie and her awaiting dessert.

Marie frowned at Holly, then quickly turned and faced the boy clown, giving him an extra big smile.

"Come over here…clown," she said, grinning, waving him over with a high pitch giggle.

Charlie pointed at himself.

"Yes, you!" she said, wearing a big grin.

Charlie's clown shoes dragged across the ground up to Marie's side.

"I kind of like you," said Marie, smiling.

Like, you've got to be kidding, thought Holly.

Before Charlie knew it, Marie's right arm lassoed around his waist, and held him tight.

Charlie's big clown smile almost melted to a pout in the clutches of Marie's arms.

"I'm going to share a bite with you—just one taste, though," said Marie.

Holly chuckled. "That's so sweet of you, rat

squeaker, but he gets killer hives if he eats so much as one strawberry. You wouldn't want him to die with an unhappy clown face… now would you?"

"I want him to tell me to my face that he's allergic to strawberries," said Marie with her eyebrows sunk low.

"He can't," said Holly.

Marie sneered. "Why Not?"

"Because he's mute, dumb, a true mime who communicates with his big smile and hands."

Marie hesitated a moment, trying to decide if she should still insist on him having a little taste. She squinted into his blank stare, then suddenly smiled. "Well, okay." Her cheeks changed from red to a cooler pink. She let loose her arm lasso around his waist, then quickly refocused her attention on the treat she was about to receive.

When Marie opened her first container of yogurt, her eyes narrowed. The surface of the yogurt wasn't flat the way she was accustomed too, but instead had mountains and valleys, appearing as if someone had been messing with her treat.

"Who? Who? Who's been in my yogurt!" shouted Marie.

Holly immediately spoke up. "For you, this yogurt has been specially whipped… specially mixed just for you. That's why it's churned," she said, leaning toward her, casting the world's biggest smile.

"Yes, I wanted it special for me!" Marie blurted. "I deserve special, whipped yogurt, just for me."

"Yes, cupcake," said Bellarouse nodding, as if she had planned it that way.

Everyone took notice that Charlie's hands were starting to twitch.

Holly quickly moved between Charlie and Bellarouse and tried to draw attention to herself. "Did you ever meet the famous twitching clown?" said Holly, in a loud cheerful voice. "Not many clowns can twitch the hula like he can."

Charlie tried to back up Holly's excuse for his nervousness by doing the best Hawaiian hula dance he could. He wasn't very good at twitching his hips and everyone noticed that too.

Marie didn't find his dance the slightest bit amusing. "Enough! Enough!" she said, refocusing her attention toward her yogurt. She looked back at her mom with her hand extended, palm faced up. "You did bring it? Didn't you?"

"Of course lemon drop," said Bellarouse, reaching into her string pearl purse to get her daughter's special silver spoon. "Here you go my precious cookie," she said.

Marie quickly dipped her spoon into the top layer of yogurt, then let a couple drops splat onto her outstretched tongue.

Holly and Charlie stood frozen, praying she wouldn't notice anything different about the taste.

Marie tilted her head to one side, then dipped her entire thumb into the container, making a nice even coating. Then, in the blink of an eye, her thumb flashed into her mouth. An expression of sheer bliss blossomed on her face. She started to smile, and her smile grew bigger and bigger until everyone could see her upper and lower teeth—gums included. Her head swept up and down with approval. She looked back at her mother. "Make sure you get the recipe for this," she chirped in a loud, unusual cheerful voice.

Minutes later, Marie finished both cases of her special treat.

Charlie and Holly nervously waited for some kind of reaction. It didn't take long. In fact, after only a couple minutes, Marie started to appear pale and drowsy. Holly didn't know for certain if her plan was going to work, but she did know that the huge amount of this new alien powder should turn her into a million times more of what she really was—a monster.

Marie's stomach started to rumble and shake. She made a loud burp, then another, and another. The whole room started to smell like strawberries.

"Oh my sweet Marie," said Bellarouse, "Are you OK?"

Marie didn't answer. The fragrance of strawberries passed through her nostrils with each burp.

Bellarouse checked her watch. "Strawberry sweet cake, We'd better get back to the circus now. The second half of the show is about ready to be served up for my gourmet daughter."

Marie slowly got up from her chair and followed Bellarouse toward the door. Halfway between the table and the exit she suddenly stopped and placed her hand up against her forehead, looking as if she was about to faint.

"Marie, pudding!" said Bellarouse, rushing to her side. She tried to hold her up as she started to wilt. "Are you okay? Your face suddenly looks… well… over baked."

Marie's entire body started to jerk back and forth. She wobbled and staggered, with her chest, face, and stomach rolling in every direction. Bellarouse grabbed her and tried to keep her steady as her hands started to swat the air every which way.

CHAPTER 27

Holly found herself face-to-face with the monster she created. Marie's true inner self started to show itself in bodily form. Her terrific anger and selfishness fueled a sudden out-of-control burst of growth. She grew bigger and bigger with each passing second, shooting up like a beanstalk, higher and higher toward the roof. The dreadful sight caused Bellarouse to faint and collapse at the base of her daughter's feet.

Marie's head started to press up against the roof with such force that the stakes anchoring the tent started to pull out of the ground. Holly and Charlie took off running across the open field.

Marie's feet sprawled out across the fairground as her body continued to shoot up like a bean stock. Bellarouse's unconscious body kept getting pushed farther and farther out in front of her feet till she was pushed over the edge of a hill. Poor Marie's mom rolled down the grassy slope and into the river. She bobbed up and down in the water, face up, and drifted downstream for about five hundred feet before she was spotted, and pulled to safety by a maintenance man on his way back from town.

* * * * *

Inside the main circus tent, the ringmaster looked up toward the ceiling as he introduced the men on the flying trapeze. Just as they started to perform, all the spectators witnessed the top of the tent start to rip open.

Four trapeze artists were shaken from their roosts and fell to the safety net below. Another trapeze performer wearing shiny white leotards saw the bar he was about to swing to suddenly lift up into the air. Looking up, he saw a monster staring down at him.

The audience beheld a horrible sight. It was Marie's face! A nightmare in any childhood dream. Little ones started to wail in their mother's arms. Parents rushed their children, grandmas and grandpas out to safety!

From the outer fringes of the fairgrounds, Holly and Charlie stared up in awe, watching Marie mushroom up higher and higher at a fantastic rate of growth. They saw families race to their cars, then drive off down the road, leaving clouds of dust behind them.

Marie's outline cloaked the sun, creating a huge shadow across the landscape. People from miles around glared up at the terrifying figure.

When Marie gazed down at the people, they reminded her of her dolls at home. She felt very powerful and had her mind set on making a lasting impression—much more than just a giant footprint. As Marie grew taller, she felt as if she could control the entire world.

"I'm a blast! A blast!" she hollered. "I will make the whole world serve me hand and foot!" Every time she spoke, the sky rumbled and quaked.

However, as the minutes ticked by, Marie became so tall, and things started to appear so small, she was afraid life would vanish as dust before her eyes.

She suddenly felt very empty and all alone. What started out as being fun and entertaining now became an hour of terror. There was panic in her voice. She cried out through the clouds, "Mom! Mom! Mom!" Her face drained of color and turned pale white, appearing like a giant white sphere. Some people looked up into the sky and thought of the moon, others a planet from outer space. Instead of craters, it glowed a huge open mouth and fiery eyes.

As Marie continued to grow, so did her appetite.

Her voice rumbled like thunder from lips that were now the size of giant blimps. "I want strawberry yogurt," she demanded. "I want strawberry yogurt now! Or I'll… I'll destroy the entire city! The country! The world! The Milky Way!" she said with cheeks now changing from moon white to Mercury red. The sun reflected off one of her silver fillings and nearly blinded a group of newspaper men trying to take pictures of the monster girl.

CHAPTER 28

Live news reports about the Claremont Circus . monster quickly spread across the country. Air shipments of strawberry yogurt were being flown in to satisfy her hunger.

Marie poked her head back through the clouds and saw railroad cars being filled with yogurt. The sight got her so excited, giant bubbles started to form from the corners of her mouth, which grew bigger and bigger till they reached the size of hot air balloons, then suddenly burst, sending thundershowers down upon the workers below. Marie grew so tall that her shoulders were now higher than the clouds.

"I'm still hungry!" she thundered. "If I don't get more strawberry yogurt, I'll… I'll, destroy the whole state!"

News of the human monster quickly reached the spaceship and Supreme Commander Zork.

"Here now," said Zork to his men, "we must

take control of this monster's mind. Go now with thirty men, hurry!"

Within minutes, the aliens formed a giant circle around Marie. All at once they beamed their mind-absorbing rays up through the clouds at the monster.

"No! It can't be!" said Charlie, seeing the circle of red beams shoot toward Marie.

"They're trying to get her mind!" said Holly.

The beams of light startled Marie. She snapped her head about and noticed that the beams were coming at her from every direction.

"What's happening?" thundered Marie. The beams of light felt ticklish and made her giggle. She noticed they were strawberry colored so she decided to reach out to try and grab one to eat. The beams tickled her all the more. Her giggling thundered and echoed across the countryside.

The aliens felt as if they were being mocked at by her laughter. Their guns weren't powerful enough. She had grown too big... too strong for their weapons to have any effect on her. After a minute, their guns started to overheat and became too hot for them to handle. They dropped them to the ground. A steamy mist rose from their guns. Minutes later, the aliens headed back to their ship.

* * * * *

Marie's appetite couldn't be satisfied. She had

a giant temper tantrum. Her arms swung wildly through the air, making the clouds appear like a giant checkerboard. As the sun beamed down through the holes in the clouds, the earth below looked like a quilt-work of alternating patches of light and shadow.

"Holly," said Charlie, peering up into the clouds from the edge of the forest. "You created a monster Frankenstein!"

"Deductively speaking, plan "A" is engaged. All we need now is for Marie to have a ghostly conscience."

"You called?" said Stephanie, suddenly appearing behind them.

"Yes, yes, called… called?" said Agatha, materializing next to her sister a second later.

Holly faced the twins. "You must convince Marie that the whole world will never be able to satisfy her hunger for very long. Tell her that the aliens are to blame. Tell her to reach down into her mother's cornfield and do a little shake, rattle, and roll. Have her demand that they leave our planet now, and never return again!"

"We will try, Miss Holly," said Stephanie, nodding.

"Yes try… try," echoed Agatha.

The twins vanished before Holly and Charlie's eyes.

Moments later, Stephanie and Agatha appeared at opposite sides of Marie's head and entered her giant ear canals. They were amazed at the size of the dark tunnels that led inside her head, measuring over eight feet in diameter.

Stephanie cupped her hands around her mouth. "Can you hear me?" she said.

"Can you hear me, me," said Agatha, echoing her voice through the opposite ear.

"Who! Who was that?" thundered Marie.

"Miss Marie, I'm your conscience," said Stephanie.

"Yes conscience, conscience!" Agatha echoed through her other ear.

Marie flung her head to the right, then the left, then quickly behind, as if expecting to see someone talking to her.

"My conscience?" said Marie, with a puzzled expression.

"Miss Marie, we know you're hungry," said Stephanie. "We want to help."

Marie slowly looked to one side, then the other, hoping the voices were just her imagination and would go away.

"Miss Marie, the aliens did this to you," said Stephanie, whispering into the dark tunnel.

"Aliens?" said Marie.

"Yes aliens… aliens," said Agatha, daring to step farther into her ear to get her message across.

"Miss Marie, they turned you into a monster and they are robbing the bodies of everyone in

Kingston!" said Stephanie. "They want the entire world next!"

"Yes, world… world," said Agatha in her loudest voice.

"I want my beautiful self back!" cried Marie. Giant tears started to roll down across her face and fell through the clouds, then burst upon the ground like giant water balloons.

"I want my mama! My home! My town!" thundered Marie.

"Miss Marie, perhaps you can help," said Stephanie.

"How?" asked Marie, looking about in every direction, still trying to figure out where the voices were coming from.

"Miss Marie," said Stephanie, "in the middle of your cornfield is a spaceship. Grab it. Shake it, but not too hard."

With the suggestion coming from her conscience, Marie leaned forward and rested her hands upon her knees. Her massive face appeared through the clouds. She gazed down into the center of her mom's cornfield, but all she could see was bare dirt.

"There's… there's nothing to grab onto."

"Miss Marie, reach out. Trust your conscience."

"Reach out," said Agatha. "Trust… trust."

Marie's hand descended hundreds of feet toward earth. With her fingers spread apart, she gripped the invisible spaceship. She smiled, feeling the saucer-like shape pressing against the inside of her palm.

Inside the spaceship, Supreme Commander Zork and his crew were suddenly shaken off their feet. The last time their ship had rocked like that was when they had been in space and got pounded by a field of meteorites. Zork waved his hand over one of his crystals. Looking up, he beheld the dark shadows cast from the underside of Marie's monstrous hand. Bands of light beamed between her fingers into his ship.

Hundreds of feet above the clouds, Marie continued to listen to what she believed to be her conscience.

"That's good, Miss Marie, now put the saucer down, gently."

"Yes, down… down," said Agatha whispering into her other ear.

Zork and his crew gazed up through his saucer at the giant girl who was staring back down at them. Her sheer size was beyond Zork's wildest dreams; a human reaching the heights of the clouds. Marie couldn't resist giving the saucer a light nudge with her foot. That moment, Zork and his crew were once again knocked off their feet.

"Miss Marie," said Stephanie, "now thunder your voice. Speak down to the place you just touched. Make demands. Tell them you will… will crush them if they don't leave now! Tell them they must leave immediately, never ever to return again!"

So Marie followed what she believed to be her conscious and thundered her voice down from the skies, demanding that the aliens leave or be smashed to pieces.

To the aliens, monster Marie was an unexpected bad dream, a sign to Supreme Commander Zork their plan had been exposed.

Through high-frequency transmission waves, all the aliens received orders from their supreme commander to leave their human bodies and return to the ship immediately. All across town human bodies started to slump to the ground. The minds of the humans trapped in the animals were set free. Minutes later, town folks started to rise again in their original bodies, and in their right state of mind.

Shortly thereafter, the alien ship blasted off into outer space.

Seconds later, the twins suddenly reappeared before Holly and Charlie.

"Miss Holly, good news!" said Stephanie with great excitement.

"Yes, yes, good news… news," said Agatha in a happy voice.

"Miss Holly! They're gone! The alien spaceship is gone!"

"Gone… gone!" echoed Agatha.

Holly and Charlie raised their arms and slapped their open palms together in a gesture of triumph over evil.

"Yes! Yes!" shouted Holly.

"I can't believe it! That crazy plan of yours actually worked," said Charlie, giving her a big hug and kiss.

"Now how are we going to get Marie back to normal?" said Charlie.

Holly thought in silence a moment. Her eyebrows suddenly arched, thinking of an idea. "Can you help us again?" she said, facing the twins.

"Yes, Miss Holly," said Stephanie. "Tell us what we must do."

"Yes… yes," Agatha echoed. "Tell us. Tell us."

"We must to try and reverse the evil monster in Marie," said Holly. "She has to think sweet, sugary thoughts. It might even make her smaller. Maybe even normal size again. It's worth a try." She pointed across the field at the last railroad container full of yogurt. "Whisper into her ear and tell her that if she were to get back to her normal size through good— happy thoughts—that last railroad car of yogurt could be her wildest dream… a swimming pool-sized serving of her favorite delight!"

The twins quickly disappeared and flew back into Marie's enormous ears to deliver the message.

"Miss Marie," said Stephanie, whispering into her left ear. "If you became normal again, that last railroad car of strawberry yogurt down there would be big enough to swim in. Imagine a huge swimming pool full of strawberry yogurt all for you!"

Marie parted the clouds with her giant hands, then peered down to earth. "But it looks so small."

"Miss Marie, if you became normal size it could be a wonderful dream… so big. Now close your eyes and dream. Dream of your heavenly swimming pool full of your favorite food," said Stephanie.

"Think happy thoughts," said Agatha into her right ear.

"I'll try, I'll try," said Marie, closing her eyes. A giant smile began to creep upon her massive face.

Suddenly, the twins were jerked off their feet. Peering out over the edge of her eardrum, they could see that Marie was getting smaller.

"Yes! That's it, Miss Marie! It's working!"

"Yes working… working!" said Agatha excitedly, jumping up and down.

The twins fled as Marie's ear canals began to close in around them, becoming smaller and smaller.

"A swimming pool full of yogurt," Marie whispered to herself. "Just for me. Just for me!"

Faster and faster she shrunk, until, moments later, she stood in the middle of the field—in her normal size.

The twins reappeared in front of Holly and Charlie.

"Miss Holly, it worked!" shouted Stephanie.

"Yes, worked… worked!" shouted Agatha.

The twins reached out and gave Holly and Charlie big hugs.

"Miss Holly, if you should ever need our help again, we will be listening for you."

"Yes listening… listening," said Agatha.

Stephanie and Agatha's face glowed from being so happy.

"Thank you, Miss Holly! Thank you Charlie," said Stephanie.

"No—thank you, for saving our families… actually our town and the whole planet," said Holly.

The twins' Great Danes suddenly appeared, looking very happy. Even their stubby tails were wagging like crazy.

"Miss Holly," said Stephanie. "They want to give you both sweet, wet, goodbye kisses."

"Oooh. That sounds nice," said Charlie taking a step back.

Mitra moved directly in front of Charlie. Spitz did the same to Holly.

"Come on, Charlie," said Holly. "We can't hurt their feelings. Let them give you a big kiss!"

"Kiss… as in gooey dog slobber?" said Charlie, still remembering the last time he got dog drool on his head while spying Bellarouse house.

"Okay… I'll go first," said Holly. She knelt down and let Spitz lick her face.

Charlie grimaced. "You're covered in saliva," he said, seeing Spitz's drool drip down across her cheek and onto the ground.

Holly gazed over at Charlie. "I can't feel it. It's ghost slobber. Quite refreshing. No residue. Trust me." Holly became a little impatient seeing him just stand there. She squinted at him. "Come on, Mitra is waiting. I bet you're kind of a celebrity guy dog's-best-friend to him."

Charlie's face cracked into a grin. "Well, I guess a little doggie facial can't be too lasting," he said, finally kneeling down. He closed his eyes and let Mitra lick his face and nose.

"See… that wasn't so bad," said Holly, smiling. "Ghost kisses tickle, don't they?"

"That's enough kisses," said Charlie, with a chuckle. He stood up and felt relieved he couldn't feel any gobs of drool anywhere.

"Miss Holly, we must depart now. I know it's so sad to go," said Stephanie.

"Yes so sad… sad," said Agatha.

Holly and Charlie each received hugs from the twins, and then said their goodbyes. They watched the twins float straight up with Mitra and Spitz prancing on thin air, circling about them as they rose higher and higher. Holly and Charlie kept waving until they disappeared into the clouds. Tears welled up in their eyes, not knowing for sure if their paths would ever cross again.

Marie walked across the open field, still in a daze from her rapid descent back to earth. Bellarouse gave her daughter a bear hug and spun her around in her arms. Next, Marie sprinted out across the field to her railroad car full of yogurt, then climbed up the side, and dove in. "I'm in strawberry heaven! Isn't it wonderful mom! Have some." She flung some yogurt off her hand and onto her mom's face.

Bellarouse suddenly shifted her attention back across the open field toward the mystery clowns that served her daughter yogurt during intermission time. She walked toward them as fast as she could, set on discovering who was beneath the makeup and clown costumes.

"Over there!" said Charlie, pointing across the open fairgrounds. "Bellarouse is heading right for us!"

"I wonder what she wants from us now?" said Holly. She gazed down the road leading back to Kingston. "There's no time to get out of these costumes. Let's split!"

"Where?"

"Back to Kingston, of course."

"As a couple of clowns?" said Charlie, watching Bellarouse pick up speed, closing in fast. "Okay, I'm right with you! Let's get going!"

Holly and Charlie took off running so fast that their giant clown shoes flew off their feet. Minutes later, people laughed and pointed out the windows of their cars at the two barefoot clowns with bouncing wigs, jogging along the highway, looking as if they didn't have it all together.

Charlie cast a big smile. "You're my number one, Holly!"

Holly blushed and took a deep breath. "You're my number one too! Without you, and all your great advice, I believe things would have turned out much different, for the worse."

Charlie and Holly stopped and gave each other a big hug and kiss.

A driver shouted out his car window as he passed by and said, "Hey, you two circus folk! Save your clowning around for the circus!"

All of a sudden, they caught sight of a patrol car heading their way.

"It's Sheriff Gary!" said Charlie.

Holly and Charlie looked at each other with blank stares. They knew that everyone should be back to normal, but they still weren't sure. Before they had time to react, Sheriff Gary pulled his patrol car to the side of the road, then quickly got out and stepped up to them.

"I tracked kids who ran off to the circus before," said the sheriff, "but this is the first time I caught a couple of clowns running away from the circus!"

Sergeant Rex popped his head out the back window and gave them a friendly howl. Instantly, Charlie somehow felt that everything was okay now and back to the good old times.

The sheriff gave them a blank stare for a moment, trying to figure out who the mystery clowns were beneath the makeup.

"It's me—Charlie Robinson… and my friend Holly, remember?"

Sheriff Gary chuckled, recognizing his voice.

"We were in Claremont… for the circus!" said Charlie. "I mean, basically, we were in it."

"Spare me the details," said Sheriff Gary. "Well, are you two clowns in need of a ride back to town?"

Holly raised her right palm. "Yeah, we could sure use one."

Holly and Charlie hopped into Sheriff Gary's patrol car. Sergeant Rex snuggled up between them in the backseat. After a short drive, they were back in Kingston.

They saw a crowd of people in front of city hall.

"I just spotted my mom and dad," said Holly. "Please, pull over!"

"You got it," said Sheriff Gary.

Holly ran toward her parents. At first, they didn't recognize the clown running right at them, and quickly stepped back.

"Mom! Dad!" shouted Holly, running toward them with outstretched arms.

"Holly?" said Phyllis recognizing her daughter's voice beneath the makeup and funny wig.

"Is that you, Holly?" said Patrick with a puzzled

look, not sure if he was seeing things.

"Yeah, you guessed it, Dad!" said Holly, giving them each a big hug and kiss. She left a funny looking red lipstick kiss mark on the side of their cheeks.

"What are you doing in that clown outfit... and coming out of that police car?" asked Patrick, looking back and forth between the car and his daughter. "Did you get into some kind trouble with the law?" he said with a look of concern.

"No, Dad, nothing like that."

Charlie stepped up to Holly in his clown outfit.

"This is my friend, Charlie," said Holly. "I never got a chance to formally introduce him to you yet."

"Your daughter played a great clown," said Charlie. "Made lots of people laugh."

"You didn't join the circus? Did you?" said Phyllis putting her hand to her forehead, looking kind of worried.

Holly grinned, "Nothing like that, Mom. No worries. We were just substitute clowns for the day, that's all," she said with her painted clown smile.

Phyllis rubbed the back of her head. "I had this terrible dream of having a really long neck like a giraffe. Isn't that crazy?"

"I had a wild dream too," said Patrick. "I dreamed I was a real swinger."

Phyllis gave Patrick a stern look.

He grinned. "Not that kind of swinger, Honey.

Like Tarzan, swinging from tree to tree. Only for some reason I had a lot more hair."

"Oh, I guess that's okay, dear," said Phyllis.

Soon, everyone was happily reunited with family and friends, and everything in and around Kingston returned back to the way it had been thanks to two super sleuths, Holly and Charlie, and the sweet Mississippi Dixie twins, Stephanie and Agatha.